The problem was right now she wasn't feeling in the slightest bit sensible or level-headed. She was feeling reckless. Wild. Weirdly out of control.

All because of Marcus—because she wanted him. God, she wanted him. Had done for years, but had always thought it one-sided. Now, though, she knew it wasn't. She could feel the attraction burning between them—fierce, mutual and utterly irresistible.

It had been so long since she'd had sex. Even longer since she'd had good sex. And with the amount of practice he'd had he'd be very good at it, she was sure.

She was under no illusions about what he was. She might have been wrong about some things, but she knew he enjoyed playing the field. She knew he didn't do commitment, didn't do long-term—which suited her fine because she didn't want either from him. She just wanted to explore this sizzling chemistry, because for one thing it would undoubtedly give her proper closure and for another who was she to fight with such a force of nature?

'Well?' he said, and the tension radiating off him suggested that he was finding it as hard to cling on to his self-control as she was.

'You know those scruples of yours?' she said, her voice low and husky.

'What about them?'

'Do they include anything concerning friends' younger sisters now?'

'Nope.'

'Good,' she said as fire licked through the blood in her veins and her heart thundered wildly. 'Then how about we finish what we started?'

Dear Reader

One of my favourite fictional relationships is that of *Much Ado About Nothing*'s Beatrice and Benedick. Ah, the 'merry war', with its wicked banter, sharp wit and biting disdain that hides something so much more... What's not to love?

So what do you get when you throw together an uptight workaholic who can't stand gorgeous laid-back charmers and a gorgeous laid-back charmer who can't stand uptight workaholics? Animosity! And when there's enough chemistry to blow up a science lab...? Sparks! Throw in a botched attempt at seduction when they were in their teens and fifteen years of denial, and it turns into a whole lot of fun.

Well, not for Marcus and Celia, perhaps—*evil laugh*—but definitely for me to write, and I hope for you to read!

Lucy x

THE BEST MAN
FOR THE JOB

BY
LUCY KING

MILLS &
BOON

Lucy King spent her formative years lost in the world of Mills & Boon® romance when she really ought to have been paying attention to her teachers. Up against sparkling heroines, gorgeous heroes and the magic of falling in love, trigonometry and absolute ablatives didn't stand a chance.

But as she couldn't live in a dream world for ever she eventually acquired a degree in languages and an eclectic collection of jobs. A stroll to the River Thames one Saturday morning led her to her very own hero. The minute she laid eyes on the hunky rower getting out of a boat, clad only in Lycra and carrying a three-metre oar as if it was a toothpick, she knew she'd met the man she was going to marry. Luckily the rower thought the same.

She will always be grateful to whatever it was that made her stop dithering and actually sit down to type Chapter One, because dreaming up her own sparkling heroines and gorgeous heroes is pretty much her idea of the perfect job.

Originally a Londoner, Lucy now lives in Spain, where she spends much of her time reading, failing to finish cryptic crosswords, and trying to convince herself that lying on the beach really *is* the best way to work.

Visit her at www.lucykingbooks.com

Other Modern Tempted™ titles by Lucy King:

ONE NIGHT WITH HER EX
THE REUNION LIE

**This and other titles by Lucy King
are available in eBook format
from www.millsandboon.co.uk**

For my editor, Megan. Thank you for
your always invaluable insight and advice!

CHAPTER ONE

TEN MINUTES AFTER the vicar had pronounced her brother and his fiancée man and wife and the register had been signed, Celia Forrester stood on the steps of the altar of the pretty Shropshire church and braced herself for the moment she'd been dreading all day.

In terms of things she'd rather not do, on a scale of one to ten, going to the gym hovered at the two mark. Pulling an all-nighter at work ranked around a four. Dinner *à deux* with her father, an eight.

Having to take Marcus Black's arm and walk down the aisle beside him, however, hit a ten.

Up until about a couple of hours ago she'd thought she'd escaped. As Dan's best friend—and consequently, best man—Marcus had been expected some time yesterday afternoon, but to the consternation of everyone apart from her he hadn't shown up. Her brother had muttered something about a missed flight and a possible arrival in time for the reception but, in all honesty, Celia had been too relieved to pay much attention.

All she'd been able to think was that she had a stay of execution and that, with any luck, by the time Marcus got there—if he got there at all—she'd have indulged in the gallon of champagne she needed to handle the horribly edgy and deeply uncomfortable effect he had on her, should she be unable to implement her customary plan A and avoid him.

She'd had no problem with following Lily—the other bridesmaid and Zoe's sister—and her brand-new fiancé, Kit, down the aisle alone. She was good at doing things alone, and she'd been more than happy about the delay in having to talk to too-gorgeous-for-his-own-good, serial womaniser and general thorn in her side Marcus Black. Quite apart from the unsettling way he made her feel, he loathed her as much as she loathed him and no doubt he would be expressing it at the first available opportunity, namely the church, so who could blame her for savouring any delay to the moment?

But then a couple of hours ago, when the three of them had been sitting in the spare room of Zoe's parents' farmhouse with rollers in their hair and tacky nails, news had reached them that Marcus had made it after all, and just like that the Get-Out-of-Jail-Free-card feeling she'd been holding onto had blown up in her face.

The degree of shock and disappointment that had rocked through her had surprised her. Then her skin had started prickling, a rush of heat had swept through her and she'd instantly felt as though she were sitting on knives.

She'd managed to hide it, of course, because firstly she was used to hiding the way he made her feel, and secondly today was a happy one that was all about Dan and Zoe and not in the slightest bit about the trouble she had with Marcus, but it had been hard. Even harder when she and Lily had entered the church behind Zoe and she'd seen him standing next to Dan at the altar, looking tall, dark and smoulderingly gorgeous in his morning suit.

But she'd done it, and she'd continue to do so because fifty pairs of eyes were trained on the proceedings and so right now she didn't have the option of giving him a cool nod and then blanking him. She was simply going to have to suck it up and accompany him down the aisle.

In approximately thirty seconds.

The organist began belting out Widor's Toccata and as Dan and Zoe turned and stepped away from the altar, their smiles wide and unstoppable, Celia pulled her shoulders back and plastered a smile of her own to her face.

She wouldn't let him get to her, she told herself, adopting the unusual strategy of channelling serenity and inner calm. She wouldn't think about the struggle she'd had throughout the ceremony resisting the constant temptation to keep looking in his direction, especially when she could feel his eyes on her. Nor would she dwell on the way that, despite her deep disapproval of him and his clear loathing of her whenever they met, he somehow managed to turn her into someone she didn't recognise, addling her brain, making a mockery of her intellect and rendering her body all soft and warm and fluttery.

No, she'd simply rise above the inconvenient and highly irritating attraction and get on with the job. She could ignore the heat of him, the mouth-watering scent of him and the invisible thread of attraction that seemed to constantly pull her towards him. She could bury the desire to drag him off somewhere quiet, press herself against him and let chemistry do its thing. Of course she could. She had done so for years, ever since the night, in fact, he'd tried to get her into bed. For a bet.

Besides, it was, what, thirty metres between the altar and the heavy oak door, so all she had to do was keep a smile on her face and her mouth shut and not let him get to her. After that, during the inevitable photo session and then the reception, which was to be mercifully short, she'd do what she always tried to do and avoid him. Simple.

Taking a deep breath and steeling herself, she glanced up at him to find him looking down at her with those wickedly glinting blue eyes that had seduced legions of women over the years.

'Shall we?' he said, a faint smile playing at the mouth that had given her an annoying number of sleepless nights over the years, as he held out his arm.

'Why not?' she said coolly, taking it.

See? This was fine. She barely noticed the hard muscles of his forearm beneath her fingers. And so what if his elbow was now pressed up against her breast and the feel of him, the heat of him, would be making her heart beat hard and fast and her body tingle if she let it? All that was relevant right now were the five stone steps she had to negotiate in heels three inches higher than she normally wore, and she needed to concentrate.

'Ready?' he asked, his deep, lazy voice tightening her stomach muscles and making her cling onto his arm a little tighter for a second. Just in case she stumbled, of course.

'Couldn't be readier.'

Reassuring herself that in five minutes or so this would all be over and she'd be free of him, Celia glanced down and lifted the longer back of her dress so it didn't catch on a heel.

'Those shoes look lethal,' he murmured as they descended the first step.

'They are.'

'And spiky.'

'That too.'

'Appropriate.'

And just like that, despite all that serenity and inner calm she'd been striving for, her intention to keep her mouth shut evaporated. 'Good of you to make it, by the way,' she said a touch acidly.

'I nearly didn't.'

'So what held you up?' she asked, once she'd safely navigated the remaining steps and could relax her grip on Marcus' arm. 'Unable to prise yourself away from an overly clingy lover? Or a pair of them perhaps? Surely it couldn't have been a trio?'

She felt him tense and wondered fleetingly if her barb had stung. Then decided it couldn't have because for one thing his many and varied bedroom exploits were no secret,

and for another they'd traded mild insults like this for years
and it had never seemed to bother him before. Nevertheless
she kind of wished it had because it would be satisfying to
know she got to him the way he got to her.

'You know something?' he said, shooting her a slow
stomach-melting smile. 'I rustled up that ash cloud especially because I knew it would wind you up.'

'My word, you literally do have a God complex,' she
said, annoyed beyond measure that he of all people should
still be the only man ever to melt any of her internal organs.
'Why am I not surprised?'

'Lucky you're always there to smack me down.'

'It's my sole purpose in life.'

'Really?' he murmured. 'I thought your sole purpose in
life was work.'

'I excel at multitasking.'

'Of course you do. Heaven forbid you should fail at anything.'

'I try not to.'

They began proceeding down the aisle at a pace that
would have had a snail overtaking them. In crackling silence, until Marcus said conversationally, 'You know, I'm
rather amazed you're here.'

Celia kept her smile firmly in place. 'Oh? Why?'

'I wouldn't have thought that you'd have been able to
drag yourself away from your desk.'

'It's my brother's wedding.'

'Nice to know there are some things that take priority.
I kept expecting your phone to go off during the service.'

She bristled and her jaw began to ache with the effort of
maintaining the smile. So she worked hard. Big deal. 'I'm
not a *complete* workaholic.' Well, not to such an extent she'd
forgo something as important as this.

'No?'

'No,' she said firmly, choosing to ignore the fact that

she *had* spent much of the morning on her phone, dealing with calls to and from the office and a string of emails that couldn't wait.

'I read about that pharmaceutical merger of yours going through. Congratulations.'

Despite the indignation Celia couldn't help feeling a stab of pride because the six months she'd spent pushing that deal through had been the toughest of her working life so far, yet she and her team had done it, and now the partnership she'd been working towards for what felt like for ever was that tiny bit closer.

'Thank you,' she said demurely, ignoring the way his body kept brushing against hers and sent thrills scurrying through her. 'And I heard you'd sold your business.' For millions, according to the gossip magazine she'd picked up and flicked through at the hairdresser's a fortnight ago, which had been light on detail about the sale and heavy on speculation about what one of London's most eligible bachelors was going to do with all his money and free time.

'I did.'

'So what are your plans now?'

'Do you really want to know?'

Not really, because she'd willingly bet her lovely two-bedroomed minimalist flat in Clerkenwell that she knew what he'd be doing for the foreseeable future. What he did best, but even better. 'I'm guessing it'll involve partying till dawn with scantily clad women.'

'Am I really that much of a cliché?'

'You tell me.'

'And spoil the fun you have baiting me?'

'You think I find it fun?'

He raised an eyebrow as he glanced down at her. 'Don't you?'

Celia thought about it for a second and decided that, as she didn't know exactly what to attribute the thrill she always got from winding him up to, 'fun' would do. 'OK, perhaps,' she conceded. 'Just a little. But no more than you do.'

'Well, I'm all for equality.'

'Yes, so the tabloids say,' she said witheringly as the interview with one of his conquests that she'd read in that magazine popped into her head. Apparently he was intense, smouldering and passionately demanding in the bedroom, and sought the same from whoever he was sharing it with. Which was something she could really have done without knowing because now she did it was alarmingly hard to put from her mind.

'You know, Celia, darling, you have such low expectations of me I find I can't help wanting to live down to them.'

Before she could work out what he meant by that he turned away and directed that devastating smile of his at a couple of women at the end of a pew on Dan's side, and as she watched them blush she mentally rolled her eyes. How very typical. That was Marcus all over. Lover of women. Literally. Lots of women.

But not her. Never her. Not that she thought about that night fifteen years ago when she'd been so desperate to lose her virginity to him. Much.

'What's with the death grip?'

Celia blinked and snapped her train of thought away from the treacherous path it would career down if she let it. 'Huh?'

'On the flowers. What did they do? What did they say? Because I know from personal experience that it doesn't take much.'

Celia glanced down at the beautiful bouquet of pink roses and baby's breath that matched her dress and saw that her knuckles were indeed white, and she mentally swore at herself for letting him get to her.

She really had to relax because if she didn't she'd never make it to the door with her nerves intact. This walk down

the aisle was taking for ever. What with the way Dan and
Zoe kept stopping to talk to people in the pews, they were
progressing at about a metre an hour and she wasn't sure
how much longer she could resist the temptation to push
past the bride and groom and make a run for it.

'The flowers haven't done anything,' she said, taking a
couple of deep calming breaths and surreptitiously rolling
her shoulders in an effort to release some of her tension.

'Am I to take it, then, that you don't really approve of
Dan and Zoe?'

Celia stilled mid-roll and stared at him for a moment, unable to work out where that had come from because Zoe was
the best thing that had ever happened to Dan, as she'd told
him after supper last night just before giving him a big hug
and wishing him luck. 'Why on earth would you think that?'

'Because you spent the entire ceremony looking like you
wished you were somewhere else.'

Oh. She hadn't wanted to be anywhere else. She'd wanted
Marcus to be somewhere else, preferably on another planet,
but she'd thought she'd managed to hide that. Clearly she'd
been wrong. 'I'm surprised you noticed.'

'Oh, I noticed,' he murmured, his gaze drifting over her
and making her skin feel all hot and tingly and tight. 'You
look beautiful, by the way.'

That was the trouble with him, she thought irritably as
she stamped out the heat with every ounce of self-control
she had. Just when she felt like slapping him, he went and
said something charming. 'Thank you.'

'You're welcome.'

'And you look very handsome,' she said, because he did
and it would be churlish to ignore the fact. More handsome
than usual if that were possible.

'My, my, a compliment,' he said softly. 'That's a first.'

'Yes, well, don't get too used to it.'

'I won't.'

They advanced another agonisingly slow couple of paces, then stopped, and he said, 'So you do approve?'

'Of Dan and Zoe?'

'Well, I know you don't approve of me.'

'I approve wholeheartedly,' said Celia with a serene smile. 'Of them.'

'They're good for each other.'

She nodded. 'They are.'

'And are your parents behaving?'

She narrowed her eyes at her parents, who were accompanying each other down the aisle in stony silence and about as far apart as it was possible to get given the width restriction of the aisle, which was pretty much par for the course. 'Just about.'

'And how's work?'

Insane. 'Work's fine.'

'Then what is there to be so tense about?'

'Tense?' she asked, blowing out a slow breath. 'Who's tense?'

'You are. If it isn't the wedding, it isn't your parents and it isn't work, I might be inclined to think it's me.'

'Hah. As if.'

Off they set again, and this time, thank heavens, it looked as though the end was in sight because Dan and Zoe had run out of guests to chat to and the great oak door was being opened and Celia could practically taste freedom.

'Admit it,' he said softly, his voice so warm and teasing that it did strange things to her stomach, 'I make you feel tense.'

'You don't make me feel anything,' she said, her pulse drumming with the need to get out of here and away from him.

'Oh, Celia, you break my heart.'

'I didn't know you had one. I thought it was another part of your anatomy entirely that kept you alive.'

'So cruel.'

'I dare say you'll survive.'

'I dare say I shall.'

And then, thank God, they stepped out into the July sunshine and she felt as if she could suddenly breathe again. She dragged in some air and blinked as her eyes became accustomed to the brightness after an hour in the church, then she took her hand from Marcus' arm and stepped away.

She didn't miss the strength of it. Or the heat of him. It was blessed relief that was sweeping through her. Of course it was, because what else could it be when the whole past ten minutes had been a nightmare she never wanted to repeat?

'Right,' she said, looking up at him with a bright smile and shading her eyes from the sun. 'Well. Thank you for that.'

'Any time.'

'So I'm going to congratulate the happy couple and mingle.' And then she was going to find the champagne and down as much of it as she could manage.

'Good idea.'

'I guess I'll see you later.'

'I guess you will.'

And with the thought that despite the conventional conversational closer hell would probably freeze before either of them sought the other out, Celia gave him a jaunty wave and off she went.

Marcus watched Celia kiss and hug her brother and new sister-in-law in turn, then laugh at something Dan said, and his eyes narrowed. Ten minutes in her company and already he was wound up like a spring. He wanted to punch something. Wrestle someone. Anything to relieve the tension that she never failed to whip up inside him.

Standing there in the warm summer sunshine while people streamed out of the church, he shoved his hands in his pockets and resisted the urge to grind his teeth because this was supposed to be a happy day and the last thing anyone wanted to see was a grim-faced best man.

But it was hard to relax when all he could think was, how the hell did Celia do it? And why?

Generally he had no trouble getting on with the opposite sex. Generally women fell over themselves for his attention and once they'd got it went out of their way to be charming. But she, well, for some reason she'd had it in for him for years and he'd never really been able to work it out.

On the odd occasion he'd pondered the anomaly, usually after one of their thankfully rare yet surprisingly irritating encounters, he'd figured that it seemed to boil down to the number and frequency of women that flitted in and out of his life, but he didn't see why that should bother her. The last time he checked it was the twenty-first century, and where he came from men and women could sleep with whomever they liked without censorship.

And so what if he enjoyed the company of women? he thought darkly, watching her peel away to take a phone call. He worked hard and he played hard. He was single and in his prime and he liked sex. He never promised more than he was willing to give and when relationships, flings, one-night stands ended there were never any hard feelings. The women he dated didn't appear to object, so who could blame him for taking advantage of the opportunities on offer?

Well, Celia could, it seemed, but why did she disapprove of him so much? Why did she care? What he got up to was none of her business. As far as he was aware he'd never hooked up with any of her friends so she couldn't have a grudge about that. And it certainly wasn't as if she were jealous. She'd made it very clear she didn't want to have anything to do with him the night he'd made a pass at her years ago and had been very firmly rebuffed.

So what was her problem? And more to the point, what

was his? What was it about her that got under his skin? Why couldn't he just ignore her the way he ignored everything he didn't need to be bothered with? Why, with her, did he always feel the urge to respond and retaliate?

Marcus sighed and pinched the bridge of his nose as the questions rattled round his head, and thought that he could really do with a glass of champagne if he stood any chance of making it through the reception.

'Is there any particular reason you're scowling at my sister?'

At the dry voice of the groom and his best friend, who'd evidently managed to drag himself away from his new wife and had stealthily materialised beside him, Marcus pulled himself together.

'Nope,' he said, snapping his gaze away from Celia and switching the scowl for his customary couldn't-give-a-toss-about-anything smile.

'Sure?'

He nodded and widened his smile because there was no way on earth he was going to let Dan in on the trouble he had with Celia. 'Quite sure. Congratulations, by the way.'

Dan grinned. 'Thanks.'

'Great ceremony.'

'The best. And thanks for being my best man.'

'No problem. I'm glad I made it in time.' He'd bust a gut over the past couple of days to get here—and whatever Celia thought it had had nothing to do with over-clingy lovers—and he might be knackered, but he wouldn't have had it any other way because he and Dan had been good friends for nearly twenty years.

'So am I,' said Dan, and then he asked, 'So why the thunderous expression? What's up?'

Marcus shrugged. 'Just trying to remember my speech.'

Dan shot him a knowing look that held more than a hint

of amusement. 'Sure you aren't ruminating about the lack of single women here?'

Oddly enough—when it was generally the first thing he ascertained at any kind of social gathering—searching for likely conquests this afternoon hadn't crossed his mind. 'Maybe a bit,' he said, largely because Dan seemed to be expecting it.

'Sorry about that, but we wanted to keep the wedding small.'

'No problem.'

'Has it been a while, then?'

'Six months.'

Dan's eyebrows shot up. 'Wow. Because of...what was her name again?'

'Noelle.' As the memory of his last girlfriend, who'd turned into a complete psycho stalker, flashed into his head he shuddered. 'And yes.'

Dan grunted in sympathy. 'I can see how after everything she did you'd be a bit wary, but, come on, six months? That must be a record.'

'Not one I'll be boasting about.'

'No,' agreed Dan. 'Why would you?'

'Quite.'

'And not one you'll be breaking today, I should think,' Dan mused.

'What makes you say that?'

'Celia's the only single woman here.'

'Is she?'

'And judging by the way you were looking at her just now I'm guessing she's not a likely target.'

Marcus inwardly recoiled. Celia? A target? As if. He couldn't stand her. And as she could stand him even less, even if he were insane/deluded/drunk enough to make a pass at her again, which he most certainly was not, in all likelihood he'd get a knee to the groin.

'Didn't we just clear that up?' he muttered, really not wanting to dwell on that particular outcome.

'Not very satisfactorily.' Dan rubbed a hand along his jaw and frowned, as if in contemplation. 'You know, Zoe mentioned she thinks you do it a lot.'

'Do what?'

'Scowl at Celia.'

'Do I?'

Dan nodded. 'Pretty much every time you come into contact, apparently.'

'Oh.'

'So what's with the two of you? Why the friction? What did she do to you?'

Interesting that Dan thought it would be that way round when everyone else would have automatically assumed he'd be the one to blame. 'She didn't do anything to me,' he said with a casual shrug. Apart from reject him. Resist him. Ignore him. Avoid him. And drive him bonkers by getting to him when he'd never had any trouble not letting her get to him before. 'We just don't get along. That's all. Sorry.'

'No. Well, she is something of an acquired taste, I'll grant you.'

One that he'd briefly acquired when he'd been an angry and out-of-control teenager but wouldn't be acquiring again, so he hmmed non-committally and sought to change the subject. 'Zoe looks radiant,' he said, watching the bride smiling and chatting, happiness shimmering all around her like some kind of corona.

'She does,' said Dan with the kind of pride in his voice Marcus couldn't ever imagine feeling, which was just as well because marriage was not for him. 'She also has a different take on it.'

'A different take on what?'

'You and Celia.'

Marcus frowned. So much for changing the subject. And

what was Dan doing, making it sound as if he and Celia were a thing when they were anything but? 'Does she?'

'Yes.'

'Right.'

'Want to know what she sees between the two of you?'

Not particularly. 'Knock yourself out.'

'Chemistry. Tension. Denial.'

Huh? Marcus reeled for a moment, then rallied because Zoe was wrong. Totally wrong. 'She sees a lot,' he said, keeping his expression poker.

'She does.'

'Too much.'

'Perhaps.'

'What makes her such an expert anyway?'

'She's made an art out of reading people. She's generally right.'

'Not this time.'

Dan shot him a shrewd look. 'She reckons it's like that kid analogy,' he said.

'What kid analogy?' asked Marcus, although he wasn't sure he wanted to know.

'The one about pulling the pigtails of the girl in class you fancy.'

At the odd spike in his pulse Marcus shifted uncomfortably. 'It's nothing like that,' he said, wondering what the hell the brief leap in his heart rate was all about.

'If you say so.'

'Celia deeply disapproves of me, and I—' He stopped because how could he tell his best friend that he thought his sister was an uptight, judgemental, workaholic pain in the arse? 'Anyway, wouldn't it bother you?' he said instead, although now he thought about it perhaps the question came fifteen years too late.

'You two together?'

Marcus nodded. 'Hypothetically speaking, of course.

I mean, she's your sister and I'm not exactly a paragon of virtue.'

'It wouldn't bother me in the slightest,' said Dan easily. 'Celia's perfectly capable of looking after herself and, actually, if I was going to issue a big-brother kind of warning I'd probably be issuing it to her.'

'Why?'

'She's a tough nut to crack.'

'One of the toughest,' Marcus agreed, because she was, and not only because she was the only nut he'd wanted but had never managed to crack. Not that he thought about that night much because, after all, it had been *years*.

'She'd drive you to drink trying.'

'Undoubtedly.'

'And that would be a shame.'

'Just as well you don't have to worry about me, then, isn't it? Although I do think you ought to be worrying about Zoe,' he added, now just wanting this oddly uncomfortable conversation to be over. 'She's been cornered by your mother and a couple of your aunts.'

'So she has,' said Dan, that smile on his face widening as his gaze landed on his wife. 'I'd better rescue her.'

'Off you go, then.'

Dan must have caught the trace of mockery in his voice because he stopped and shot him a look. 'One of these days it's going to happen to you, you know.'

'What is?'

'Love and marriage.'

Marcus shook his head and laughed. 'Not a chance.' He valued his freedom far too much, and anyway, he'd seen what love could do. The pain it could bring. The tragedy it could result in. He'd been part of the fallout.

Dan arched an eyebrow. 'Too many women, too little time?'

'You said it.'

'If you really believe that then you're going to end up like my father, heading for sixty and still chasing anything in a skirt.'

'That's a risk I'm prepared to take.'

Dan laughed and clapped him on the back. 'One day, my friend, one day,' he said, then set off for Zoe, leaving Marcus standing there frowning at Celia and thinking, Chemistry, tension and denial? What a load of crap.

CHAPTER TWO

THREE HOURS LATER, Celia had worked her way through one cup of tea, two glasses of champagne, a dozen of the most scrumptious mini sandwiches and petit fours she'd ever eaten and a hefty piece of wedding cake. She'd survived the photo session, listened to the short yet witty speeches, and had had conversations with everyone except Marcus and her father.

The reception so far had been beautiful. The weather was behaving, the sky a cloudless blue, the sun beating down gently, a perfect example of one of those heavenly yet rare English summer days. Zoe's parents' garden, with its immaculate lawn, colourful and fragrant borders and sharply clipped hedges was an idyllic setting for a small, tasteful, traditional wedding celebration. The music coming from the string quartet sitting beneath the gazebo drifted languidly through the warm air and mingled with the happy hum of chatter, so enchanting and irresistible that every now and then couples came together and swayed along.

She had to admit that, even to an unsentimental person such as herself, the romance of the afternoon was undeniable. She could feel it winding through her, softening the hard-boiled parts of her a little and making her feel uncharacteristically dreamy. Even her parents seemed to have been caught up in it, appearing to have reached a sort of unspoken truce and, although not talking, no longer shooting daggers at each other from opposite ends of the garden. Her brother looked happier than she'd ever seen him and his bride sparkled like the champagne that had been flow-ing so wonderfully freely.

Yet as mellow as she was feeling and as much as she liked her brand-new sister-in-law, Celia couldn't help wishing Zoe were more of a people person. If she were, there'd have been several hundred guests at the reception instead of the fifty or so that were milling around the garden.

And OK, so as bridesmaid and sister of the groom she wouldn't have been able to wriggle out of the photo session either way and she'd still have had to steel herself against the weight and strength of Marcus' arm around her waist and the heat of his hand on her hip as they posed, but at least she'd have been able to ignore him after that.

As it was, though, guests were thin on the ground and she couldn't be more aware of him. Everywhere she looked there he was in her peripheral vision, smiling and chatting and generally making a mockery of her efforts to blank him from her head.

Despite the fact that she'd positioned herself about as far from him as possible, for some reason, he was utterly impossible to ignore. Not that she hadn't tried, because she had. A lot. In fact, she'd used up practically all of her men-tal and emotional energy trying, and as a result she hadn't really been able to concentrate on anything. She kept los-ing track of conversations. Kept finding herself gravitating towards him. Every time she told herself to get a grip and hauled herself back on track his laugh would punctuate the air and she'd have to battle the urge to whip her head round to see what was amusing him.

All afternoon the people she'd been talking to had looked at her closely and asked if she was all right before edging off presumably in search of less ditzy company, and she re-ally couldn't blame them.

It was driving her nuts. She abhorred ditz. And she hated the way she was being so easily distracted now when she'd always prided herself on her single-mindedness and her ability to focus.

Why was she having such trouble with the effect Marcus had on her today when she generally managed to keep it under control? Why couldn't she blank him out as she usually did? Why did she keep trying to get a glimpse of him whenever she heard the sound of his voice, and then sighing wistfully when she did?

What was wrong with her? What was this weird sort of ache in her chest? And more importantly right now, she thought, her attention switching abruptly from Marcus and the strange effect he was having on her equilibrium, how was she going to deflect her father, who'd clearly clocked the fact that she was on her own and was bearing down on her, no doubt intending to launch into his usual spiel about her career, her lack of a husband and the direct correlation between the two?

As the pathetic—and pointless—need for his approval surged up inside her the way it always did and briefly smothered her confusion at the way her emotions were running riot this afternoon, Celia cast around for a conversation to join, a guest to corner, anything to avoid him and his own particular brand of paternalism, but she was on her own. The nearest little group contained Marcus, who unbeknownst to her had circulated into her vicinity and from the sounds of it was entertaining for Britain, and that made it a no-no.

Or did it?

As her brain raced through the very limited options open to her Celia made a snap decision. Oh, what the hell? He might not be her greatest fan but Marcus was within grabbing distance, and nothing could be worse than having to suffer her father's prehistoric ideas and deep disappointment when it came to his one and only daughter.

Aware that her father was fast approaching and there was no time to lose, Celia reached out and clamped her hand on

Marcus' arm. He went still, then turned, surprise flickering across his face. Ignoring the sizzle that shot through her from the contact, Celia looked up at him in what she hoped was a beseeching fashion and said softly, 'Help me? Please?'

Well, well, well, thought Marcus, glancing down to where she was clutching his arm and then shifting his gaze to her face, which bore a sort of pleading expression he'd never have associated with her. Who'd have thought? Celia Forrester, a control freak extraordinaire, staunchly independent and so uptight she was in danger of shattering, a damsel in distress. Actually asking for help. *His* help. She must be desperate.

Resisting the temptation to shake his head in astonishment, he excused himself from the people he'd been talking to, intrigued despite himself by the urgency in her voice and the despair in her expression. 'Why? What's up?' he asked.

'My father.'

He flicked a glance over her shoulder and saw that Jim Forrester was indeed making a beeline for her. And it was making her jumpy. Which wasn't entirely surprising. 'I see,' he murmured with a nod. 'What help do you want?

'I need small talk.'

'What's it worth?'

She stared at him for a second. 'What do you mean, what's it worth?'

He grinned because had she really expected him not to take full advantage of having the upper hand? 'Exactly that.'

She narrowed her eyes at him. 'What do you suggest?'

'How about asking me nicely? Then again. And again.'

She gaped. Then snapped her mouth shut and frowned. 'You want me to beg?'

His smile deepened at her discomfort and he had to admit that there was something rather appealing about having Celia in his debt with this brief and strictly one-off foray into chivalry, should he agree to it. 'The idea has merit, don't you think?'

She glared at him, her eyes flashing with indignation, but a second later the attitude had gone and she shrugged. 'Fine,' she said flatly as she started to turn away. 'Forget it. You go back to doing whatever you were doing. I can handle Dad.'

And for some reason Marcus found himself inwardly cursing while now feeling like the biggest jerk on the planet. She might be a pain in the neck, but he knew how difficult she found her father and he knew how much she loathed *him,* which meant that she *was* desperate.

And maybe a little vulnerable.

'Look, sorry,' he muttered, frowning slightly at the flare of a weird and deeply unwelcome kind of protective streak, because Celia was the last person who needed protecting and the last person he'd ever consider vulnerable. 'I can do small talk.'

She stopped mid-turn and looked up at him. 'Really?'

'Of course.'

'What do you want in return?'

'Nothing.'

She arched an eyebrow sceptically, switching back to the Celia he knew and could handle. 'Seriously?' she said.

'Seriously.'

'Then thank you,' she said a bit grudgingly, which he supposed was only fair.

'You're welcome.'

'Celia,' boomed her father behind her and he saw her jump. Wince. Brace herself.

But she recovered remarkably well and after taking a deep breath turned and lifted her cheek for her father's kiss. 'Dad, you remember Marcus Black, don't you?' she said, stepping back to include him in the conversation.

'Of course,' said Jim Forrester, flashing him a smile that

was probably calculated to be charming but in a couple of years could easily stray into sleazy, and holding out his hand. 'How are you?'

'Good, thanks,' said Marcus, shaking it and then letting it go. 'You?'

'Excellent. Great speech.'

'Thank you.'

'So how's business?'

'Quiet.'

Jim's eyebrows shot up. 'I heard it was doing well. So what happened? Hard times?'

He smiled as he thought of the relief he'd felt when he'd signed those papers and released himself from the company that he'd devoted so much of his time and energy to. 'Couldn't be better.'

'Marcus sold his business, Dad,' said Celia.

'Oh, did you? Why?'

'The thrill of beating the markets had worn off,' he said, remembering the strange day when he'd sat down in his office, stared at the trading screen flickering with ever-changing figures and, for the first time since he'd set up the business, just couldn't be bothered. 'It was time to move on.'

'You burnt out,' said Celia, looking at him in dawning astonishment, as if she couldn't believe he was capable of working hard enough to reach that stage.

'Nope,' he said. 'I decided to get out before I did.'

'So what are your plans now?' asked Jim.

'I have a few things in the pipeline. Some angel investing. Some business mentoring. I'd also like to set up a kind of scooping-up scheme for able kids who slip through the system and are heading off the rails, which gives them opportunities other people might not.'

He caught the flash of surprise that flickered across Celia's face and a stab of satisfaction shot through him. That's right, darling, he thought dryly. Not partying till dawn with scantily clad women. At least, not only that. And perhaps not every night.

'Philanthropic,' said Jim with a nod of approval. 'Admirable.'

It wasn't particularly. It was just that he'd been given a chance when he'd badly needed it and he simply wanted to pay it forward. 'I've done well,' he said with an easy shrug, 'and I'd like to give something back.'

'Let me know if I can help in any way.'

Jim had a divorce law practice so it was doubtful, but one never knew. 'I will, thanks.'

'I'm up for partnership, Dad,' said Celia, and Marcus thought her voice held a note of challenge as well as pride.

'Are you?' said her father, sounding as if he couldn't be less interested.

'I'll know in a few months.'

'That's all very well and good,' Jim said even more dismissively, 'but shouldn't you be thinking about settling down?'

Marcus felt Celia stiffen at his side, and guessed that this was a well-trodden and not particularly welcome conversation. 'I enjoy my job, Dad,' she said with a sigh.

Her father let out a derisive snort. 'Job? Hah. What nonsense. Corporate lawyer indeed. There are enough lawyers already, and I should know. You should be married. Homemaking or whatever it is that women do. Giving me grandchildren.'

Dimly aware that this was in danger of veering away from small talk and into conversational territory into which he did not want to venture, moment of chivalry or no moment of chivalry, Marcus inwardly winced because, while he hadn't seen Celia's father for a good few years, now it was coming back to him that as far as unreconstructed males went one would be pushed to find one as unreconstructed as Jim.

Going on what Dan had said over the years their father had never had much time for Celia's considerable intellect or any belief in her education, as had been proven when Dan had been sent to the excellent private school Marcus had met him at while she'd been sent to the local, failing comprehensive.

Now it was clear that Jim had no respect for the choices she'd made or the work she did either, but then over the years Marcus had got the impression that the man didn't have much respect for women in general, least of all his wife and daughter. He certainly didn't listen to either.

'And one day I'd like to be doing exactly that,' she said, pulling her shoulders back and lifting her chin, 'but there's still plenty of time.'

'Not that much time,' said Jim brutally. 'You're thirty-one and you haven't had a boyfriend for years.'

Celia flinched but didn't back down. 'Ouch. Thanks for that, Dad.'

'How are you ever going to meet anyone if all you do is work? I blame that ambition of yours.'

'If my ambition is to blame then it's your fault,' she muttered cryptically, but before Marcus could ask what she meant Jim suddenly swung round and fixed him with a flinty look that he didn't like one little bit.

'You married?' he asked.

Marcus instinctively tensed because for some reason he got the impression that this wasn't merely a polite enquiry into his marital status. 'No.'

'Girlfriend?'

'Not at the moment.'

'Then couldn't you sort her out?' said Jim, with a jerk of his head in his daughter's direction.

Celia gasped, her jaw practically hitting the ground. 'Dad!'

Marcus nearly swallowed his tongue. 'What?' he managed, barely able to believe that this man had basically just pimped out his daughter. In front of her.

'Take her in hand and sort her out,' Jim said again with the tact and sensitivity of a charging bull. 'Soften her up a bit. You have a reputation for being good at that and with the business gone and your future projects not yet up and running you must have time on your hands.'

'Stop it,' breathed Celia, red in the face and clearly—and understandably—mortified.

Not that Marcus was focusing much on her outraged mortification at the moment. He was too busy feeling as if he'd been hit over the head with a lead pipe. He was reeling. Stunned. Although not with dismay at Jim's suggestion. No. He was reeling because an image of taking Celia into his arms and softening her up in the best way he knew had slammed into his head, making his pulse race, his mouth go dry and his temperature rocket.

Suddenly all he could think about was hauling her into his arms and kissing her until she was melting and panting and begging him to take her to bed, and where the hell that had come from he had no idea because she didn't need sorting out. By anyone. Least of all him. And even if he tried he'd probably get a slap to the face.

God.

Running his finger along the inside of his collar, which now felt strangely tight, Marcus tried to get a grip on his imagination and keep his focus on the conversation instead of the woman standing next to him. The woman who couldn't stand him.

'I don't think that's a very good idea,' he muttered hoarsely and cleared his throat.

'Of course it isn't a good idea,' said Celia hotly.

'Why not?' said Jim with an accusatory scowl, as if he, Marcus, was being deliberately uncooperative. 'She might be a bit of a ball-breaker but she's not bad-looking.'

'Hello?' said Celia, waving a hand in front of her father's face. 'I am here, you know.'

Marcus knew. Oh, he knew. And not just that she was only a foot away. It was as if Jim had unlocked a cupboard in his head and everything he'd stuffed in there was suddenly spilling out in one great chaotic mess.

To begin with, not bad-looking? *Not bad-looking?* That was the understatement of the century. She was gorgeous. All long wavy blond hair, eyes the colour of the Mediterranean, full pink lips and creamy skin. A tall hourglass figure that made his hands itch with the need to touch her. A soft, gorgeous, curvy exterior behind which lay a mind like a steel trap, a drive that rivalled his own and a take-no-prisoners attitude that was frighteningly awesome.

Today, in a pink strapless dress and those gold high-heeled sandals with her hair all big and tousled and her make-up dark and sultry, she looked absolutely incredible. Sexy. Smouldering. And uncharacteristically sex kittenish.

It was kind of astonishing he hadn't noticed before. Or maybe subconsciously he had. The minute she'd walked into the church and he'd laid eyes on her, hadn't everyone else pretty much disappeared? Hadn't it taken every drop of his self-control to keep his jaw up, his feet from moving and his mind on the job?

With hindsight it was a miracle he'd managed to get down that aisle without dragging her off into the vestry. He'd felt her touch right through the thick barathea of his sleeve and it had singed his skin and tightened every muscle in his body. The scent of her had scrambled his brain and the proximity of her had heated his blood. As for the pressure of her breast against his elbow, well, the lust that that had aroused in him had nearly brought him to his knees.

If he hadn't been so deeply in denial he'd have had bad, *bad* thoughts about her. In a church, for heaven's sake.

He'd told himself that it was exhaustion messing with

his head, which, come to think of it, was the excuse he always made when it came to the irrational and inappropriate
thoughts of her that occasionally flitted through his mind.

But it wasn't exhaustion. It was denial, pure and simple. Because how could he be so in thrall to someone who
clearly didn't feel the same way about him? How could he
be so weak?

So was *that* what bothered him so much about her, then?
The one-sided attraction and the back-seat position it put
him in? Was the fact that he'd never stopped wanting her
the reason why the way she constantly judged him and always found him lacking pissed him off so much?

Despite what she thought of him he fancied the pants
off her, which meant that, despite his protests to the contrary earlier, Zoe had been right. On his side at least, there
was chemistry, tension and, up until about a minute ago, a
whole heap of denial.

And as denial was now apparently not an option he might
as well admit that her rejection of him still stung despite
the fact that it had happened years ago. She was the one
who had got away, and that was why she got to him, why
he always retaliated when she launched an attack on him.

'So what do you think?' said Jim, interrupting the jum-
ble of thoughts tangling in his head. 'Would you be up for
the challenge?'

'He thinks you're insane, Dad,' said Celia fiercely. 'And
so do I. I know I'm a disappointment to you but, for goodness' sake, this has to stop. Now.'

Actually, with the realisation that he wanted her, what
Marcus thought was that he was suddenly bone-deep tired
of the animosity that she treated him with. It had been going
on for years, and he was sick of not knowing what it was
about or where it came from.

After spending so long in denial it was surprising just
how clearly he could see now. His vision was crystal, and

he wanted answers. So whether she liked it or not he was
going to get them before the afternoon was through.

'Want to go and get a drink?' he muttered, figuring that
there was no time like the present and that with any luck
she'd consider him the lesser of the two evils in her vicinity right now.

'I thought you'd never ask.'

CHAPTER THREE

OH, GOD, THOUGHT CELIA, lifting her hands to her cheeks and feeling them burn as she abandoned her horror of a father and trailed in Marcus' wake. How on earth was she going to recover from this? Would she *ever* get over the mortification and the humiliation? Not to mention the mileage that Marcus would get out of that disaster of a conversation. Her father might not know it but he'd given him ammunition to last him *years*.

How *could* he have suggested she needed sorting out? She'd always known he didn't have much time for her career and that he thought she ought to be stuck in a kitchen, barefoot and pregnant, but he'd never expressed it so publicly before.

And in front of Marcus of all people.

What must he be thinking?

Well, no doubt she'd be finding out soon enough because given their history what were the chances he'd let such a scoop slide? Practically zero, she thought darkly as a fresh wave of mortification swept through her. He probably couldn't wait to get started.

But that was fine. She'd survive whatever taunts he threw her way. She always did. And this time she didn't really have any choice, as she'd known the minute she'd elected to go with him instead of staying with her father. She'd made the split-second decision on the basis that by actually living in the twenty-first century Marcus was the marginally more acceptable of the two, but with hindsight maybe she should have just fled to the bathroom instead and to hell with the weakness that that would have displayed.

As they reached the bar Celia pulled herself together because she had the feeling that she'd need every drop of self-possession that she had for the impending fallout of what had just happened.

'What would you like?' he asked.

'Something strong,' she said, not caring one little bit that it was only five in the afternoon. She needed the fortification. 'Brandy, please.'

'Ice?'

Diluted? Hah. 'No, thanks.'

Marcus gave the order to the barman and the minute she had the glass in her fingers she tossed the lot of it down her throat. And winced and shook her head as the alcohol burned through her system. 'God.'

He watched her, his eyes dark and inscrutable, and Celia set her glass on the bar and kind of wished he'd just get on with it because her stomach was churning and she was feeling a bit giddy.

Although now she thought about it his eyes lacked the glint of sardonic amusement he usually treated her to and his face was devoid of the couldn't-care-less expression it normally wore when they met. In fact she got the odd impression that he wasn't thinking about her father or that conversation at all, which made her think that perhaps he wasn't planning to launch a mocking attack on the pathetic state of her love life just yet.

So what *was* he going to do? And more to the point, what was *she* going to do, because she could hardly stand here looking at him for ever, could she? Even though deep down she wouldn't mind doing just that because he was, after all, extremely easy on the eye.

A rogue flame of heat licked through her and she wondered not for the first time what things would be like be-

tween them if the antagonism didn't exist. Kind of secretly
wished it didn't because he was still looking at her as if trying to imprint every detail of her face onto his memory, and
every cell of her body was now straining to get up close and
personal to him and the effort of resisting was just about
wiping out what was left of her strength.

'Want to take a seat for a bit?' he murmured, and she
snapped out of it because, honestly, what was *wrong* with
her today?

Deeply irritated by her inability to control either her
thoughts or her body, Celia pulled herself together and focused. Yes, she'd just had a pretty uncomfortable experience, but what was she, eighty? Besides, she was on edge
and restless, as if a million bees were swarming inside her,
and she needed to lose the feeling. 'I'm going to take a
walk,' she said, gripping the edge of the bar and bending
down to undo her shoes.

'I'll join you.'

No way. 'I'd rather be alone.'

'I'd like to talk to you.'

She glanced up. 'What about?'

'You'll see.'

'No, I won't.'

He tilted his head and smiled faintly. 'Don't you think
you owe me for helping you out back there?'

Had he helped her out? She didn't think so, although that
wasn't his fault. 'I thought you said you didn't want anything in return for your help.'

'Humour me.'

Straightening and dangling her shoes from the fingers of
one hand, Celia didn't see why she should humour him in
the slightest, but maybe it wasn't such a bad idea because
on reflection she'd made some pretty inaccurate assumptions about him today. Therefore she owed him at least one
apology, and it would probably be less humiliating to do that

on the move when she'd have an excuse to keep her eyes on the ground on the lookout for random tree roots waiting to trip her up.

'OK, then,' she said coolly. 'Let's walk.'

'This way?' he said, gesturing in the direction of the walled kitchen garden that would at least afford them privacy for the talk he wanted to have and the apology she had to give.

'Fine.'

They set off across the lawn and as the chatter of the guests and the music faded Celia felt her coolness ebb and her awareness of him increase. He was so tall, so broad and so solid and every time his arm accidentally brushed hers it threw up a rash of goosebumps over her skin and sent shivers down her spine.

She sorely regretted taking off her shoes. They might be tricky to walk in, particularly over grass, but they'd added inches. Without them she felt strangely small despite the fact that she was well above average height, and a bit vulnerable, which, as she was the least vulnerable person she knew, was as ridiculous as it was disconcerting.

She tried to distract herself by mentally formulating an apology that would let her keep at least a smidgeon of dignity, but it was no use. She couldn't concentrate on anything except the man walking beside her. There was something so different about him at the moment. He seemed unusually tense. Controlled. Restrained. Maybe even a bit dangerous...

Which was utterly absurd, she told herself firmly, shaking her head free of the notion. Not to mention idiotically fanciful. Marcus wasn't dangerous. No. The only danger here was her because with every step she took away from the safety of the crowd she could feel the pressure inside her building and her self-control slipping.

'You can relax, you know,' he murmured, shooting her

a quick smile that flipped her stomach and unsettled her even more.

Suddenly totally unable to figure out how to handle the situation, she fell back on the way she'd always dealt with him and shot him a scathing look. 'No, I can't.'

'Why not?'

'You have to ask?'

'Clearly.'

She stopped. Planted a hand on her hip and glared at him, all the tension and confusion whipping around inside her suddenly spilling over. 'Oh, for goodness' sake, just get on with it, Marcus.'

'Get on with what?' he asked, drawing to a halt himself, a picture of bewildered innocence.

'The "talk" you wanted to have. Come on, you must be dying to gloat about the sorry state of my love life, not to mention all the other things my father said.'

He thrust his hands in his pockets and looked at her steadily. 'I'm not going to do that.'

She rolled her eyes. 'Yeah, right. Why change the habit of a lifetime?'

Marcus pulled his hands from his pockets and shoved them through his hair while sighing deeply. 'Look, Celia,' he said, folding his arms across his chest and pinning her to the spot with his dark gaze. 'How about we try a cease-fire on the hostilities front?'

For a moment she just stared at him because where on earth had that come from? 'A ceasefire?' she echoed, as taken aback as if he'd grabbed her and kissed her. 'Why?'

'Because I'm sick of it.'

She blinked, now blindsided by the weariness in his voice as well. 'You're sick of it?'

'Aren't you?'

She opened her mouth to tell him she wasn't. But then she closed it because hadn't she been wishing the animosity between them didn't exist only minutes ago? 'Maybe,' she conceded. 'A bit.'

'I suggest a truce.'

'And how long do you think that would last? Five minutes?'

'Let's try and give it at least ten.'

'For the duration of the "talk"?'

'If you like.' He tilted his head and arched a quizzical eyebrow. 'Think you could do that?'

Celia didn't really know what to think. A ceasefire? A truce? Really? Was it even possible after fifteen years of animosity?

Maybe it was. If Marcus was willing. She could be civil, couldn't she? She generally was. So with a bit of effort she could manage it now. Particularly since, despite herself, she was kind of intrigued to know what he wanted to talk to her about. And besides, she didn't like the way he was making her sound like the unreasonable one here. She wasn't unreasonable at all, and she'd prove it.

'Why not?' she said, tossing him a cool smile from over her shoulder and continuing towards the kitchen garden.

Well, that had gone a lot more easily than he'd expected, thought Marcus, going after her. He'd anticipated much more of a battle, much more withering sarcasm and scathing retort, but then perhaps that conversation with her father had knocked her confidence a bit. Not that she'd ever dream of showing it, of course.

Nevertheless a mortified, confidence-knocked Celia was novel. Intriguing. More alluring than it probably should have been. As was a chat without all the acrimony, he reminded himself swiftly, which was the main point of this little exercise.

'So I'm imagining that wasn't quite the way you were

intending the conversation with your father to go when you asked for my help,' he said once he'd caught up with her.

Celia snapped her gaze to his and shot him a look of absolute horror. 'Not exactly.'

'So much for small talk.'

She shook her head as if remembering the conversation in all its awful glory, and winced. 'I still can't believe he said all that stuff about, well, you know, sorting me out and things.'

'Nor can I.' Although, to be honest, he was now so aware of her, it was pretty much all he could think about. That and getting to the bottom of why she detested him so much.

'I'm so sorry.'

'Why? It's not your fault.'

'I guess not, but, still, he put you in an awkward position.'

'I doubt mine was as awkward as yours.'

'Probably not.'

'Nor is it your fault your father's stuck in the Dark Ages.'

'No, but that doesn't make it any easier to bear.'

They reached the kitchen garden and he held open the gate. Celia brushed past him, making all the nerve endings in his body fizz and his pulse race as her scent slammed into him.

'Where does it come from?' he asked, just about resisting the urge to take advantage of her proximity and pulling her into his arms because that was not what this was about.

'His attitude?'

He nodded and followed her down the path that bisected the garden, watching the sway of her body that was exaggerated by the flimsy fabric of her dress and ignoring the punch of lust that hit him square in the stomach.

Celia shrugged and sighed, then bent to look at the label stuck in the earth in front of a row of something leafy and green. Her hair tumbled down in long golden waves and

Marcus found himself scanning the garden for a soft piece of ground he could pull her down to.

'Who knows?' she said, and he dragged his attention back to what she was saying. 'The fact that he was a doted-on only child? That he had a stereotypical fifties mother? Or was he simply born a chauvinist?'

'Why do you put up with it?' he said, clearing his throat and determinedly shoving aside the images of Celia writhing and panting beneath him, her dress ruched up around her hips and her body arching against him.

She straightened, swept her hair back with a twist and looked at him. 'I don't have any choice. He's still my father even though I'm never going to be what he thinks I should be.'

'Which is no bad thing,' he said, briefly trying to imagine Celia as a housewife and failing.

'I agree. I can't cook. I don't have a clue where my iron is and I haven't used a Hoover since my last day at university.'

'Yet you still want his approval?'

She nodded. 'Stupidly. I always have. Although I really don't know why I still bother. I mean, he barely knows you yet he admires you in a way he's never admired me even though he's known me for thirty-one years. We work in similar fields, for goodness' sake, yet he's never offered *me* help. Whatever I achieve he'll never think it amounts to as much as marriage and a family would. Which is ironic, really, when you think about how badly he screwed his up.'

'Is his attitude to women why your parents divorced?'

She shook her head. 'I think that was mainly because of his many, *many* affairs. But the attitude couldn't have helped.'

'So what did you mean when you said your ambition was his fault?'

'Exactly that. The divorce hit me hard. Despite what he'd done I adored him. When he moved out I spent quite a lot of my time at school pathetically crying in the bathrooms. As a result I was bullied.'

That odd protective streak surged up inside him again and he frowned. 'Badly?' he asked, pushing it back.

'Not really. Small-scale stuff. But one day I'd had enough and decided to channel my energies into studying instead of blubbing my eyes out.'

'Is it a coincidence you're a lawyer?'

She arched an eyebrow and shot him a quick smile. 'What do you think?'

'I think Freud would have a field day.'

'Very probably.'

'But why corporate law? Why not divorce law?'

'Experiencing it once—even though sort of vicariously—was quite enough,' she said with a shudder.

Marcus watched her as she began to walk further along the path and thought that, while he did think she had a problem with her work-life balance, her drive and focus when it came to her career were admirable. She'd worked hard and deserved everything she had. 'What you've achieved is impressive,' he said, reaching her with a couple of long, quick strides. 'Especially with so little encouragement.'

She glanced over at him, surprised. 'Thanks.'

'You deserve everything you have.'

'Wow,' she said slowly. 'I never thought I'd hear you say that.'

'Neither did I.'

They continued in silence for a moment. Celia brushed her hand over a planter full of lavender and a faint smile curved her lips, presumably at the scent released.

'Anyway, you haven't always had it easy, have you?' she said.

'No,' he said, although he'd got over the death of his parents and the trouble he'd subsequently had years ago.

'So you've done pretty impressively too.'

Funny how the compliment warmed him. The novelty of a sign of approval after so many years of the opposite. Or maybe it was just the sun beating down on the thick fabric of his coat. 'Thanks,' he muttered.

She turned to look at him and her expression was questioning. 'Why am I telling you all this anyway?'

'I have no idea.'

'Must be the brandy.'

'Must be.'

'I don't need sorting out, you know.'

'Of course you don't.'

'I don't need rescuing.'

'I know.'

She shot him a quick smile. 'I definitely don't need to see my father for at least a decade.'

'A century, I should think.'

At the fountain that sat in the middle of the garden they turned left and carried on strolling down the path, passing raspberry nets and then runner-bean vines that wound up tall, narrow bamboo teepees before stopping at a bench that sat at the end of the path amidst the runner beans.

'I'm sorry, Marcus,' she said eventually.

He frowned, not needing her continued apology and not really liking it because, honestly, he preferred her fighting. 'So you said.'

'No, not about that,' she said with a wave of her hand. 'I mean about the things I implied you were going to do with your time now you'd sold your business. It was totally childish of me to suggest that you'd be partying with floozies. Your plans sound great. Different. Interesting.'

'I hope they will be.'

'I was wrong about that and I was probably wrong about why you were late getting here too, wasn't I?'

'Yup.'

'No trio of clingy lovers?'

'Not even one.'

'Shame.'

'It was.'

'So what happened?'

'I was in Switzerland tying up a few last details sur-rounding the sale of my company but was due to fly back yesterday morning. I should have had plenty of time, but because of the ash cloud my flight was cancelled, as were hundreds of others. By the time I got round to checking, all the trains were fully booked and there wasn't a car left to rent for all the cash in Switzerland.'

'What did you do?'

'Found a taxi driver who drove me to Calais. From there I got on the train to cross the Channel, rented a car in Dover and drove straight here.'

'Oh.' Celia frowned. 'When did you sleep?'

'I didn't.'

'You must be tired.'

Oddly enough he wasn't in the least bit tired. Right now he was about as awake and alert as he'd ever been. 'It's not the first time I've gone twenty-four hours and I doubt it'll be the last.'

'You're very loyal.'

'Dan's my best friend. Why wouldn't I be?'

She shrugged and carried on looking at a point in the distance so that, he assumed, she didn't have to look at him. 'Well, you know…'

Something that felt a bit like hurt stabbed him in the chest but he dismissed it because he didn't do hurt. 'Maybe I'm not everything you think I am,' he said quietly.

She swivelled her gaze back to his and sighed. 'Maybe you aren't.'

'Just what did I do, Celia?'

'What do you mean?'

'Why the hatred?'

'I don't hate you.'

He lifted an eyebrow. 'No? Seems that way to me. You never pass up an opportunity to have a go at me. You judge me and find me lacking. Every time we meet. Every single time. So what I want to know is, what did I ever do to earn your disdain?'

She frowned, then smiled faintly. 'I've just told you about my father's relentless philandering and the misery it caused,' she said with a mildness that he didn't believe for a second. 'Can't you work it out?'

Ah, so it boiled down to the women he went out with. As he'd always suspected. But he wasn't going to accept it. It simply wasn't a good enough reason to justify her attitude towards him.

'Yes, I date a lot of women,' he said, keeping his voice steady and devoid of any of the annoyance he felt. 'But so what? All of them are over the age of consent. I don't break up marriages and I don't hurt anyone. So is that really what it's all been about? Because if it is, to be honest I find it pretty pathetic.' He stopped. Frowned. 'And frankly why do you even care what I do?'

Celia stared at him, her mouth opening then closing. She ran a hand through her hair. Took a breath and blew it out slowly. Then she nodded, lifted her chin a little and said, 'OK, you know what, you're right,' she said. 'It's not just that.'

'Then what's the problem?'

'Do you really want to know?'

'I wouldn't have asked if I didn't.'

'Well, how about you trying to get me into bed for a bet?' she said flatly. 'Is that a reasonable enough excuse for you?'

Marcus stared at her, the distant sounds of chatter and music over the wall fading further as all his focus zoomed in on the woman standing in front of him, looking at him in challenge, cross, all fired up and maybe a bit hurt.

'What?' he managed. What bet? What the hell was she talking about?

'The bet, Marcus,' she said witheringly, folding her arms beneath her breasts and drawing his attention to her chest for a second. 'You set about seducing me for a bet.'

As he dragged his gaze up to the flush on her face her words filtered through the haze of desire that filled his head and he began to reel. '*That's* what's been bothering you all these years?' he said, barely able to believe it. '*That's* what's been behind the insults, the sarcastic comments and the endless judgement?'

She nodded. Shrugged. 'I know it sounds pathetic but that kind of thing can make an impression on a sixteen-year-old girl.'

An impression that lasted quite a bit longer than adolescence by the looks of it, he thought, rubbing a hand along his jaw as he gave himself a quick mental shake to clear his head. 'You should have told me.'

'When exactly?'

'Any point in the last fifteen years would have been good.'

She let out a sharp laugh. 'Right. Because that wouldn't have been embarrassing.' She tilted her head, her chin still up and her expression still challenging. 'In any case, why should I have told you?'

'Because I'd have told you that there wasn't a bet.'

She frowned. 'What?'

'There wasn't a bet.'

'Yeah, right.'

'Really. I swear.'

She stared at him and the seconds ticked by as she absorbed the truth of it. 'Then why did you say there was?'

Marcus inwardly winced at the memory of his arrogant, reckless, out-of-control and hurting teenage self. 'Bravado.'

'Bravado?'

'I was eighteen. Thought I knew it all. When you pushed me away it stung. Battered my pride. It hadn't happened before.'

'I can imagine,' she said dryly.

'Your knock-back hit me hard.'

'I find that difficult to believe.'

'Believe it.'

'You called me a prick-tease.'

Marcus flinched. Had he? Not his finest moment, but then there hadn't been many fine moments at that point in his life. 'I'm sorry. I wanted you badly. You seemed to want me equally badly. And then you didn't. One minute you were all over me, the next you basically told me to get off you and then shot out through the door.'

'It wasn't entirely like that.'

'No? Then what was it like? Why did you stop me that night?'

'I was a virgin. I got carried away. And then I suddenly realised I didn't want to lose my virginity to someone who'd probably be in bed with someone else the following night.'

'I might not have been.'

Celia rolled her eyes. 'Yeah, sure.'

And actually, there was no point denying it, she might well be right. At eighteen, with the death of his father six months before and his mother's all-consuming grief that had left no room for a son who'd been equally devastated, and ultimately no room for life, he'd been off the rails for a while. The night of Dan's eighteenth birthday party, which had fallen on the anniversary of the date his father had been diagnosed with pancreatic cancer, he'd been on a mission to self-destruct, and he hadn't cared who'd got caught up in the process. In retrospect Celia had had a lucky escape. 'Well, I guess we'll never know.'

'I guess we won't.'

'I was pretty keen on you, though,' he said reflectively.

'Were you?'

'Yup. Even though you were Dan's sister and therefore strictly off-limits.'

'Not that off-limits,' she said tartly. 'If I hadn't put a stop to things we'd have ended up in bed.'

'No, well, I didn't have many scruples back then.' As evinced by the fact that following Celia's rejection he hadn't wasted any time in finding someone else to keep him company that night.

'And you do now?'

'A few. And you know something else?' he said, taking the fact that she was still standing there, listening, as an encouraging sign.

'What?'

'Despite everything that's happened between us over the years it turns out I still am pretty keen on you.'

CHAPTER FOUR

JUST WHEN CELIA didn't think she could take any more shocks to the system, bam, there was another one.

She was still trying to get her head around the fact that Marcus thought that what she'd achieved with her career was impressive. That she'd got quite a large part of him badly, *badly* wrong. That there'd never been a bet and the enormity of what that meant. That ever since that night her attitude towards him—and men in general—had been fuelled by one tiny misunderstanding and could have been so very different if teenage angst hadn't got in the way.

So, on top of all that, the news that he wanted her was too much for her poor overloaded brain to take.

'What?' she said, rubbing her temple with her free hand as if that might somehow remove the ache that was now hammering at her skull.

'I want you,' he said, taking a step towards her and battering her senses with his proximity. 'A lot. I think I always have.'

'You have an odd way of showing it,' she said, edging back a little and feeling the pressure inside her ease a fraction.

The look in his eyes, dark and glittering and entirely focused on her, made her stomach flip. 'I don't take rejection well,' he said softly.

'No, you don't.'

'And you haven't exactly been encouraging.'

'Why would I be?'

'You wouldn't. Yet despite that you're the sexiest woman I've ever met.'

Celia swallowed hard and tried to keep things rational because this was Marcus and he had the patter nailed, but it was hard to think straight when she wanted to be anything but rational. 'Has it occurred to you that I might simply be the one that got away?'

'Yes.'

'And?'

'Does it matter?'

Did it? She didn't have a clue about anything right now except for the desire sweeping through her. 'I guess that depends on what happens next.'

'What do you want to happen next?'

'I don't know.'

But she did. Because if she was honest it was what she'd wanted for years now, even though she'd done her best to bury it. Hadn't she been wishing that the animosity between them would abate? Hadn't she been wondering what would remain if it did? Hadn't she had hot, steamy dreams about it?

And now it seemed as if the ill will had gone, and she didn't have to wonder what would remain any more because she could feel it. Right down to her marrow. Electricity. Excitement and want. Unfettered by the past. Unleashed by the present.

He took a step towards her, then reached out and ran his hand from her shoulder slowly, so slowly down her arm, watching as he did so.

'You really don't know?' he murmured and she shivered.

'Still working on it,' she said, because what with the speed this was going, what with the whiplash one-eighty their relationship had undergone, some kind of caution here seemed prudent.

'Did you know your sister-in-law thinks we have chemistry?' he said softly, his fingers circling her wrist and resting over her thundering pulse.

'I didn't.' But it didn't surprise her because Zoe was perceptive like that.

'She thinks there's tension.'

'There's certainly been that.'

'Apparently she also thinks we're in denial.'

'Right,' she said weakly because she could barely breathe with the lust slamming through her, let alone speak.

'Although I'm not any more.'

Celia swallowed and thought that, seeing as how Marcus was being brutally honest at the moment, what else could she do but return the courtesy? 'I never have been,' she murmured.

'No?'

'I've always been attracted to you. I haven't wanted to be. It's been driving me insane.'

His jaw tightened. His eyes darkened. He twined his fingers through hers and tugged her closer and her heart began to thump wildly.

'So what do you suggest we do about it?' he said softly, so close that he dazzled her. Scrambled her thoughts. Melted her brain. Rendered her all soft and mushy inside.

Nothing was one option. The sensible one probably and definitely the one that would cause her the least emotional upheaval.

But Celia had been sensible all her life and look where it had got her. She had a great career and pots of cash in the bank, but while her friends were tripping over themselves to rush up the aisle, as her father had so thoughtfully pointed out, she hadn't had a boyfriend in years.

Which generally suited her fine. She didn't want a serious relationship right now. With the prospect of partnership on the horizon she didn't have the time or the energy needed to devote to one. Yet, this afternoon, for the first time in months, she'd been aware of how alone she was.

A medley of images now spun through the fog in her head: Dan and Zoe smiling adoringly at each other as they cut the cake; the look she'd caught Lily and Kit exchange during the speeches, a look that held love, acceptance, hope and such heat; all those couples swaying to the music.

And her. Standing alone moments before her father had sought her out, her chest squeezing with loneliness and envy.

The irony was that if it hadn't been for Marcus' stupid bravado her relationship history for the past fifteen years could have been very different. She might not have been so wary of men. She might not have been so suspicious of their motives. She might not have scared off anyone who showed more than a passing interest in her. She might even have eased up a bit on her career in order to have a relationship. A marriage. A family.

But what was the point of dwelling on that now? She couldn't change the past. And she was happy with her life. Today's stab of loneliness was nothing more than a blip. Tomorrow she'd be back in London, back at work, and she'd be fine.

She was glad she and Marcus had the opportunity to clear the air. It gave her some sort of closure. Maybe once the deal she was working on was out of the way she might be able to start a whole new chapter of her life romance-wise. Maybe she'd stop pushing men away. Maybe she'd find someone who was as driven as she was, who held the same values she did. Someone as sensible and level-headed as she was.

The problem was, right now, she wasn't feeling in the slightest bit sensible or level-headed. She was feeling reckless. Wild. Weirdly out of control. Her body was behaving way beyond its remit. Emotions were churning through her and playing havoc with her common sense.

All because of Marcus, because she wanted him. God,

she wanted him. Had for years, but had always thought it one-sided. Now, though, she knew it wasn't, and she could feel the attraction burning between them, fierce, mutual and utterly irresistible.

It had been so long since she'd had sex. Even longer since she'd had good sex. And with the amount of practice he'd had he'd be very good at it, she was sure.

She was under no illusions about what he was. She might have been wrong about some things, but she knew he enjoyed playing the field. She knew he didn't do commitment, didn't do long-term, which suited her fine because she didn't want either from him. She just wanted to explore this sizzling chemistry because for one thing it would undoubtedly give her proper closure and for another who was she to fight with such a force of nature?

Mind made up, Celia ignored the little voice inside her head telling her she was mad and dragged her gaze up from the expanse of his chest. She saw a muscle in his jaw begin to pound and his eyes darken, and desire flooded through her.

'Well?' he said, the tension radiating off him suggesting that he was finding it as hard to cling onto his self-control as she was.

'You know those scruples of yours?' she said, her voice weirdly low and husky.

'What about them?'

'Do they include anything concerning friends' younger sisters now?'

'Nope.'

'Good,' she said as fire licked through the blood in her veins and her heart thundered wildly. 'Then how about we finish what we started?'

One quick tug was all it took and then Celia was flush against him, her eyes widening and her lips parting on a gasp, although what she thought she was surprised about Marcus had no idea.

What did she think would happen when she'd basically just told him she wanted to have sex with him? He might not have acknowledged it before but he'd been waiting for this for fifteen years. He wasn't going to wait one more second. Couldn't anyway, because the heat and want now flaring in the depths of her eyes, so different from the disdain and disapproval he was used to, were seducing him so completely that everything faded but her.

What did he care about the wisdom of this? The implications? The potential fallout? He couldn't even think about any of that. Not when the soft, pliant feel of her against him and the thready sound of her breathing, altogether such a contrast to her usual smart-talking, insult-delivering toughness, were obliterating what remained of his self-control.

All he cared about right now was the fact that her dislike of him had been largely based on a misunderstanding, and despite all the odds against such a thing happening she was in his arms. Gazing up at him. Waiting for him to kiss her.

So he did. As anticipation thundered through him he lowered his head and covered her mouth with his. Tongues touched and at the bolt of electricity that shot the length of his body he nearly lost his mind.

As instinct took over and wiped his brain he disentangled his fingers from hers and slipped his hand to the small of her back. He slid his other hand up her arm to the nape of her neck and then buried it in her hair, holding her head steady as he increased the pressure, deepened the kiss.

Celia moaned and pressed herself closer, sort of sinking into him. He heard the thud of her shoes and her bag hitting the path, and then her arms were round his neck, threading through his hair, and her soft breasts pushed harder against his chest, as if she needed the pressure, was desperate for the friction.

When he drew back after what felt like hours but could only have been a minute or two, she looked dazed, her eyes all unfocused, her face flushed and her breathing ragged. Which pretty much mirrored the way he was feeling.

'You pack quite a punch,' he murmured, thinking with the one brain cell that was working that if he'd known they'd generate this much heat he'd have ignored the sarcasm and put her mouth to better use long ago.

'So do you,' she said shakily. 'But if someone had told me this morning that I'd be kissing you now I'd have had them sectioned.'

'It's not exactly the outcome to the afternoon I'd have predicted either,' he said, his heart racing and the blood pounding through his veins.

'You mean this wasn't what you meant by a ceasefire in hostilities?'

'Not exactly.'

'An interesting turn of events, then.'

And about to get even more interesting, if things went his way, which he intended them to because this kind of combustible compatibility shouldn't be allowed to go to waste.

'Very,' he said, pulling her tighter and leaving her in no doubt of how much he desired her.

He felt her tremble and it sent a reciprocal tremble shuddering through him. 'What exactly do you want, Marcus?' she breathed.

'You. Here.'

'Now?' She shivered in his arms, the idea clearly appealing if the way her pupils were dilating was anything to go by.

'Now.' There'd be time for finesse later. They had all night for long and slow. He just wanted her and he wasn't sure how much longer he could last.

'Flattering,' she breathed with a faint smile.

'At this point, desperate.'

'Same here.'

'So?'

The flush on her cheeks deepened, her breath caught in her throat and her eyes darkened. 'Be careful of the dress,' she murmured and he felt like punching the air in victory.

'I will,' he said instead and brought his mouth down on hers once again.

This time they didn't stop to talk. Hands roamed everywhere, their bodies pressed together tightly; they only broke apart to take in great gulps of air before kissing again.

So hard and tightly wound he wasn't sure he could stand it much longer, Marcus slid his hands over her hips, down, and then round, delving beneath her dress and finding warm, smooth skin. He swept his hand up her thigh, felt her tremble against him, and then he was cupping the hot centre of her through fine, silky lace.

Celia tore her mouth from his and dropped her head back, letting out a soft moan when he tilted her pelvis up and slid first one finger into her and then another. So hot and wet, so tight, instantly clamping around him as if she intended to never let him go.

He moved his fingers inside her. He stroked. Slid in and out. Found her clitoris with his thumb and teased. And all the while trailing his mouth along her jaw, down her neck and over her collarbone.

She clutched his shoulders and arched against him, whimpering and panting. Her hips jerked and he could feel her tightening around him. And then she moved her hands to his head, yanking it up and pulling it forwards, planting her mouth on his to smother her moan as she came, shaking in his arms, convulsing around his fingers and making him burn with the need to be inside her.

Shudders racked her body and she kissed him wildly as she rode it out, and then she was tearing her mouth away, breathing hard as she grappled with the button of his trousers and unzipped his fly, slipping her hand inside.

The minute she touched him, Marcus lost it, the desperation to bury himself in her as deep as he could overwhelming all logical thought and reason. He reached behind him, searching for the tiny hidden pocket in the lining of one of the tails, in which he'd stashed a condom months ago, which took longer than usual because his hands were shaking so much.

Not least because Celia was thrusting her hands beneath the waistband of his shorts and pushing them and his trousers down. She wrapped her fingers around him and moaned faintly, and he gripped her wrist and yanked her hand away before he exploded. He tore open the packet with his teeth, shook away the foil and, dimly remembering her concern about her dress, whipped her round.

He swiftly rolled the condom on, grimacing with the effort to control himself, then he bent her forwards and positioned her hands wide apart on the back of the bench. He lifted the back of her dress, rolling it up to her waist in the vague, distant hope that that would stop it creasing. He put his hands on her waist, slid them down over her hips. Tore at one side of her knickers, then the other, and the fabric floated to the ground. He pushed one knee between her legs, parting them. And then, holding her steady, he drove into her.

She was hot and wet and tight and felt like velvet, and he felt his self-control unravel.

With a soft groan she arched her back and threw her head back. She pushed back, and ground against him, and Marcus lost his battle to keep this clean. Leaning over her and wrapping a hand in her hair, he brought her head up and lowered his so that his mouth was close to her ear, and he started telling her what he wanted to do to her, how she felt.

She moaned again and mumbled something that sounded

a lot like 'hurry' and he began thrusting in and out of her, harder and faster, all animal instinct and primitive need, until he could hear her breathing turn ragged, could see her knuckles go white as she clung onto the bench, could feel her tightening around him, squeezing him and wiping his mind of everything but her and the yearning for release clawing at his insides.

The pressure within him built. The heat surged like wildfire. She spread her legs wider, rotated her hips faster and ground against him harder. Then he felt her tense, heard her take a breath, and somehow, despite the haze of desire in his head and the hammering of his heart and the roaring in his ears, he untangled his hand from her hair, whipped it round and clamped it over her mouth a second before she came.

Her harsh, muffled cry and the feel of her unravelling around him shot him over the edge, and, pulling her back, he drove into her hard and fierce, and with a scorching rush of heat and a surge of blinding white pleasure he lodged deep and emptied himself into her.

His heart was thundering so frantically and his head was spinning so fast he didn't hear the ringing of a phone at first. But he did feel her jolt. Squirm. Shake her head free of his hand.

And it snapped him to. Enough, at least, to figure out the noise was coming from the tiny bag she'd dropped to the ground.

'Leave it,' he said gruffly, not wanting to let her go just yet and so strengthening his hold on her.

'I can't,' she said, her voice hoarse as she tried to wriggle out of his grip. 'It might be important.'

'So's this.' Because for some reason he had the feeling he ought to apologise. Ask if he'd hurt her with his roughness.

'*This* is finished,' she muttered, pushing him back with her bottom and then jerking forwards and freeing herself from him.

Still reeling from the intensity of the experience and oddly weak-limbed, Marcus felt the loss of her heat immediately. But even though he'd like nothing more than to drag her to the ground and do that all over again, although this time face to face and to hell with her dress, what could he do but take his hands off her? Wherever it had been a minute or two ago, her mind was now clearly on the call coming in, and he swore softly because there went the opportunity to apologise.

While Celia hastily shoved her dress down in a way that undid all the care he'd taken with it earlier and then dived for her bag and delved inside for her phone, Marcus dealt with the condom, his mind blitzed. As she turned away and walked off, talking into her phone and clearly not happy about something, he had nothing left to do but think.

For the first time in his life he had no idea what he was going to say once she finished the call. He didn't have a line. Didn't have a protocol because he'd never had scorching sex with someone who only about an hour ago had loathed him.

So what happened now? he wondered, watching her frown then throw her hand in the air, frustrated by the conversation. Where did they go from here? Back to the insults? Back to the hostility? A new kind of awkwardness? Or was this the beginning of something different, something faintly intriguing?

Marcus frowned and stalked back, taking a moment to pick up Celia's knickers, balling them up and shoving them in his pocket because the sight of those in the bin might give the gardener a bit of a fright come Monday morning.

Did he want something different? Something intriguing? He shouldn't, but did he? Did she? Right now, with his heart still beating fast, his body still thrumming with the lingering effects of his climax and his head a mess, he didn't have a clue. The only thing he did know was that, whatever Celia might think, this wasn't finished. Not by a long shot.

CHAPTER FIVE

'CELIA! THERE YOU ARE! Thank God.'

At the voice that rang out behind her Celia nearly jumped a mile in the air and spun round to see Lily, her fellow bridesmaid, striding towards her, although what she was needed for she had no idea because as far as she was aware her bridesmaid's duties had ended a while ago.

But then, right now she had no idea about anything. Five minutes after what had just happened, what she and Marcus had just done, and she was still totally adrift. Her heart was still thundering, her body still buzzing and, having had less than a minute to think about it, her brain a mess trying to process it all.

How on earth had it happened?

One minute they'd been kissing, the next she'd been shattering first in his embrace, then over the bench, and loving all of it. Aware of her femininity and feeling powerful in a way she never had before, she'd revelled in the intensity, the desperation she could sense in him and the feel of being enveloped and then possessed by him.

And what the hell was that all about anyway? Since when had she wanted to be possessed? Since never was the answer to that because in her opinion being possessed by a man smacked of submission, and submissive was something she'd never been.

But then this afternoon had been full of new experiences. She'd never gone from a kiss to sex and then to it all being over so fast. The whole thing had lasted, what, maybe five, ten minutes? And as for the foreplay and the sweet-talking that she usually enjoyed, well, that had been practically non-existent.

Mind you, perhaps it hadn't been all that fast. Perhaps there'd been fifteen years of foreplay. And perhaps she wasn't as into sweet-talking as she'd always thought, because she certainly hadn't minded the filthy things he'd muttered in her ear as he leaned over her.

But who knew why she'd lost all self-control like that? She certainly didn't. After two of the most mind-blowing orgasms she'd ever had she could barely think straight, and Lord only knew what nonsense she'd spluttered to Annie, her secretary, who'd been calling about a document that was urgently needed by her boss but was missing.

Anyway, with Lily fast approaching, why what had just happened had happened wasn't something she had time to consider. Which was actually quite a relief because she had the feeling that it was probably a bigger deal than she was able to cope with right now.

All she could think of doing was wiping the past ten minutes from her mind and applying one hundred per cent of her focus on Lily. So she snapped her phone shut, fixed a smile to her face and tried not to think about the fact that she wasn't wearing any knickers.

'Lily,' she said, sounding mercifully normal even though inside she was chaos. 'What's up?'

'I've been looking for you all over the place,' said Lily with the breathlessness of someone who'd been running. 'And then your phone rang and I thought I recognised the ringtone.'

'How lucky,' she said, although what was really lucky was that Lily hadn't found her ten minutes ago.

'What are you doing here all by yourself?'

'She's not here all by herself.'

Celia's mouth went dry and her heart lurched at the realisation that Marcus was behind her. Again. Although this time hopefully fully dressed and not bending over her. Not that she was going to think about him thrusting inside her, how deep he'd been, how good it had felt…

As heat rushed through her and a wave of desire nearly wiped out her knees Celia felt her cheeks burn, silently swore and gave herself a quick mental shake.

'Oh,' said Lily slowly, swinging her gaze from Celia to Marcus and then grinning knowingly. 'I see.'

'We've been chatting,' said Celia, blushing even more hotly and obviously sounding as guilty as sin.

Slowly returning her attention to Celia, Lily gave her a quick once-over, her gaze lingering on her burning face, her hair that was no doubt all over the place, her crumpled dress and her lack of shoes. 'If you say so.'

'I do,' she said, rallying her strength and shooting her co-bridesmaid a look that had quelled many an argumentative client, but merely made Lily grin.

'Well, whatever you were planning on doing next,' she said breezily, 'you're going to have to put it on hold because Dan and Zoe are about to leave and there's a bouquet that needs to be thrown.'

At the thought of that, all heat vanished and Celia stiffened, then groaned, closed her eyes and pinched the bridge of her nose. 'Oh, God,' she muttered as the implication of the bouquet-throwing part of the day suddenly struck her. 'Like I need any more humiliation today.'

'What's humiliating about a bunch of flowers flying through the air?' asked Marcus dryly, sounding so laid-back and unaffected by having just had her over a bench it made her nerves jangle.

'You wouldn't understand,' she said, turning and looking at him and then wishing she hadn't because her gaze locked on his mouth and all she could think about was those deep drugging kisses and the not-so-sweet nothings he'd growled into her ear.

'Try me.'

She dragged her gaze up and that was even worse because traces of heat and desire lingered in his eyes, reminding her of what she really was trying to forget. 'You can't. You will never have to experience the mortification I'm about to suffer,' she said, knowing she was going to sound pathetic and wishing she'd just nodded and gone with Lily without saying anything. 'I'm the only single girl here. Everyone else is married. I'll have to stand there alone and everyone will be watching. Wait until you see the looks being cast my way—which will range from smug to pitying—and then you'll see.'

Marcus tilted his head and looked at her intently, as if spotting a crack in her armour and trying to see through it. Not that he'd find anything even if he could, apart maybe from a horseshoe magnet with both its ends quivering in his direction.

'You're not the only single girl here,' he said, rubbing his fingers along his jaw, and she couldn't help watching, remembering how they'd felt inside her. 'There's Lily.'

'She's engaged,' she said, wondering where the hell her inner strength and self-control were when she needed them. 'Doesn't count.'

'Sadly, this is true,' said Lily thoughtfully.

'Then I'll join you,' he said.

Celia stared at him. What? No. She didn't need him being all nice on top of the fabulous sex. That really would screw with her head. 'Sorry?'

'I'll join you. Hustle you for the bouquet.'

'You?'

'Why not? I'm single. And, actually, technically so are you, Lily, despite being engaged. And while we're at it why don't we recruit Kit? That might make it a bit more of a battle.'

'A novel idea,' said Lily with a grin. 'I'll go and get him. So, are you coming?'

This she said to Celia, who thought that she already had. Deliciously. Twice. In the space of about five minutes. 'Absolutely,' she said, wishing she could give herself a good kick. 'Give me a moment to put on my shoes.' And find her underwear, regain her composure and exert some sort of control over her brain.

'Great.'

Celia watched Lily lift her dress and rush off, and muttered, 'You're mad,' in Marcus' general direction.

'Probably,' he said, thrusting his hands in his pockets, at which point his jaw tightened and his dark eyes glittered. 'You can thank me later if you like.'

Celia hmmed non-committally because she wasn't sure if his plan was going to make things better or worse, stalked over to the bench and scoured the ground. 'Where the hell are my knickers?'

'In my pocket.'

'Can I have them back, please?'

'Not really much point.'

'Why not?'

Colour slashed along his cheekbones as he gave her the kind of smile that suggested he was enjoying a memory. 'There's not much left of them.'

'Oh.'

He tilted his head and his smile widened, becoming wicked. 'Don't you remember me ripping them off you?'

Celia bit her lip and felt her blush deepen. She'd been so lost in desire and desperation she hadn't felt anything except the deep hammering urge to have him inside her. 'I forget the details,' she said a little huskily.

'I don't think I'll ever forget any of the details. I think they'll for ever be burned into my memory. That was hotter than I'd ever have imagined. You're hotter than I'd ever have imagined.'

Celia really didn't know what to say to that. 'Thank you. And thank you for suggesting the bouquet thing,' she added, deeming it wise to get off the subject of hotness and the circumstances surrounding it.

'You're welcome. But you should know my motives aren't entirely altruistic.'

'No?'

Marcus shook his head and looked down at her, his eyes burning right through her. 'It occurred to me that the sooner Dan and Zoe leave, the sooner we can.'

He might not yet know it but Celia wasn't going anywhere with Marcus.

Now that the heat and the recklessness of her behaviour in the kitchen garden had faded, reality had struck with the force of a mile-high pile of legal documents hitting her desk.

What the hell had she done back there? What had she been *thinking?*

Well, she hadn't been thinking at all, that much was clear. Because if she had, she'd have considered the fact that they'd effectively been in public. That fifty or so people had been within spitting—*hearing*—distance. That a dozen security people—thanks to Dan's high profile and his deep dislike of the press—had been monitoring the perimeters of the garden, on the lookout for gatecrashers and long lenses and possibly even couples having wild sex amongst the vegetables.

If someone had discovered them…

Dear God. It didn't bear thinking about. Quite apart from eternal humiliation and probably being the subject of rumours for years to come, she could have been fired. Her partnership prospects would have been history. She could have been struck off for bringing her profession into disrepute. Her father would have been beside himself with the

knowledge that Marcus had followed up on the suggestion
that he sort her out.

And OK, so none of that had happened, but the fact still
remained that at some point shortly after walking into that
garden with him she'd *completely lost her mind.* A couple of hot and heavy kisses and she'd abandoned the self-
control she valued so highly. For the first time in her life
she'd given in to the needs of her body. Without a single
moment's consideration. He'd given her an out, given her
a chance to put a stop to things, and all she'd said was, 'Be
careful of the dress.'

Be careful of the flipping *dress.*

As if he could do anything he wanted with her and all
that mattered was that she looked presentable afterwards.

Not that she'd even managed that. Her hair was a mess
and her face was still burning—although hopefully if anyone noticed they'd assume it had something to do with the
hideousness of standing in the drive with Lily, Kit and Marcus while Zoe smiled widely, turned and, to the cheer of the
guests, tossed the bouquet high into the air.

And as for her lack of underwear... Well, even though
technically it wasn't her fault, who went commando at a
wedding where there was the possibility of a breeze or an
ignominious fall to the ground courtesy of four-inch heels?

It was as if she'd been taken over by someone else today.
Someone who wasn't cool and collected and totally un-
flappable, but tense and jumpy and chaotic. Someone who
was ruled by emotion instead of reason. Someone who did
things like have sex in the open air with a thoroughly un-
suitable man.

And now all those things that had seemed so exciting
half an hour ago—the recklessness, the loss of control, the
overwhelming desire to slake the clawing lust—now just
seemed wrong. Shameful somehow.

Even though physically she'd adored what she and Marcus had done—who was she to deny the fabulousness of two earth-shattering orgasms in quick succession?—she was beginning to realise that she'd just become one of his conquests. One in a very long line of women he'd taken to bed and then forgotten about. Not that there'd been a bed involved, but still.

It shouldn't really have mattered, but, annoyingly enough, it did. Because while she was under no illusion about him, maybe by assuming a quickie with Marcus would deal with the attraction she felt for him, she'd been under an illusion about herself. She'd had a better time with him than she'd expected to. Hadn't thought that kind of pleasure actually existed. Was kind of knocked sideways by the fact that it did, and that she'd experienced it. And while she'd never fall for the mistake of thinking she could be the one to re-form him, even if she wanted to, which she didn't, if she hung around she could well find herself wanting more instead of closure.

Given everything she'd endured today and the way her emotions had got the better of her it wasn't entirely surprising. Her confidence and her self-belief had been bashed. Things she'd always thought she'd known had been proved false. And as for her emotions, well, those were all over the place.

But however justifiable her behaviour today had been she still didn't like it. She didn't know what it meant. Didn't have the energy to work it out.

Nor did she have the energy for the night of heaven Marcus was no doubt planning, tempting though her body clearly thought it was. She needed space, time and distance to figure out that today was nothing more than a blip, that the sex, even though spectacular, had been just that and that she'd be back to normal in a jiffy.

So, all in all, she thought, watching the bouquet sail

through the air and land in Marcus' hands, it was lucky she'd booked herself on the seven-o'clock train back to London.

God only knew where the suggestion he join Celia in the drive for the throwing of the bouquet had come from. All Marcus knew was that he'd caught that flash of vulnerability again and he'd found himself wondering how the hell he could have ever thought her uptight and judgemental when she clearly had a core of marshmallow. A deeply hidden core of marshmallow, admittedly, but there nevertheless.

And as a result of the glimpse he'd got of it, he was now waving goodbye to Dan and Zoe, who were heading off on a two-month honeymoon in South America in a vintage convertible, while clutching a bunch of pale pink roses and feeling a bit of a berk. But he reckoned he could live with that. Especially if it meant that Celia felt obliged to express her gratitude for his chivalry in bed later.

As his pulse began to race at the thought of the long, hot, steamy night ahead, during which he'd make sure she expressed her gratitude over and over again, Marcus wondered if she'd be up for meeting up once back in London.

Now that they'd lost the hostility he wouldn't mind getting to know her a bit better. He might have been acquainted with her for close on the twenty years he'd known Dan, but he didn't really have a clue how she worked. As an adolescent he hadn't been interested, at eighteen he'd just wanted to get into her pants and as an adult the animosity had acted as a barrier to thinking of her as anything but a thorn in his side. Now, though, he was thinking he'd quite like to find out.

Which was odd because up to this point he'd never really wanted to explore the minds of the women he'd dated. It wasn't that he didn't think they'd be all that interesting. In fact, he was sure they would be, because he didn't date bimbos. The women he went out with were bright and entertaining, yet despite that he'd just never been sufficiently engaged to want to try to dig all that far beneath the surface, even with those who lasted weeks instead of only one night. He didn't really know why this was, it was just the way it had always been.

Celia, however, intrigued him. Her mind, her work ethic, her ambition and her drive as much as the spectacular body beneath the dress. With hindsight she always had fascinated him, even when she'd been needling him. Maybe *particularly* when she'd been needling him. And he didn't really know the reason for that either.

What he *did* know, however, was that he'd like to see more of her. Literally, of course, because he still hadn't seen her naked, but also because this thing between them deserved a lot more exploration.

And while anything long-term clearly wasn't an option when they had polar-opposite views on marriage and family, that didn't mean that if she was up for it they couldn't have some fun in the meantime, did it?

In fact, why wait till later? he thought, lowering his hand and vaguely wondering if it would be all right to just dump the flowers on the ground as his heart began to thump. Why not whisk her away now as he'd implied earlier he wanted to? She was right there, standing beside him and waving as the car headed down the drive. What could be quicker than sending her up to get her stuff and then dragging her off to his hotel? Or hers. He wasn't fussy.

'So another couple bites the dust,' he murmured, deciding as he watched the red brake lights disappear round the corner that etiquette probably took as dim a view of abandoning the bouquet as Celia would of him throwing her over his shoulder and carting her off.

'In a cloud of dust,' she said, screwing her face up in disgust and now flapping her hand in front of her face to wave it away. 'Do you mind?'

'What about?'

'Your best friend's just got married,' she said. 'Your re-lationship will change.'

Contemplating the idea, Marcus figured that Celia was probably right about that, although he wasn't unduly wor-ried. It wasn't as if he and Dan saw each other all the time. They met up once, maybe twice a month at the most, and he couldn't see why that should change. 'Zoe doesn't strike me as the sort of woman who'd ban her husband from see-ing his friends,' he said.

'No. She's lovely. And I think they're going to be very happy.'

This she said with what he would have thought was a trace of wistfulness if it had been anyone other than Celia, but, because it *was* Celia, she was probably not consider-ing her own happiness but the way *her* relationship with her brother would change.

But then to his faint alarm she sighed deeply, and he shot her a quick glance only to find a kind of dreamy expression on her face that he'd never have expected.

'Are you all right?' he asked, not sure quite what to make of it.

'Fine,' she said, giving herself a quick shake and smiling at him brightly—too brightly, perhaps. 'You?'

'Never felt better.' Oddly enough, it was true. He might not have slept in the past twenty-four hours but he felt great. Amazing the effect some seriously wild, uninhibited, un-expected sex could have on a man...

'Congratulations, by the way,' she said, her smile still fixed in place, her eyes oddly unreadable.

'What for?'

'That,' she said, glancing down at the bunch of flow-ers he was still, for some unfathomable reason, holding. 'It means you're next.'

Marcus gave a theatrical shudder to mask the less theatrical one he felt deep inside. 'Hell will freeze over first,' he muttered.

'Then you really shouldn't have caught it.'

'I like to win.' And he had, even though Kit and Lily had put up an excellent good-natured battle. Celia, come to think of it, hadn't put up any kind of a fight. She'd just stood there looking as if she'd been miles away.

'And what will you do when word gets out? You'll be swamped.'

'I'll use you as my shield.'

She tilted her head and looked at him sceptically. 'Meaning what exactly?'

Who knew? All he knew was that as long as they had mileage, and they clearly did what with the electricity that was bouncing back and forth between them, he'd be pursuing it. 'Meaning go and get your things, Celia, and say your goodbyes.'

'I'm just about to.'

'Good.'

She took a deep breath and pulled her shoulders back, her smile fading a little. 'About us leaving together, Marcus...'

'What about it?'

'We won't be.'

That was fair enough. Her parents were here and he could understand her desire for discretion. He was perfectly happy for them to leave separately and meet up later. 'Fine,' he said easily. 'Where were you planning on staying tonight?'

'At home.'

He went still at that. Frowned. 'What?'

'I'm heading home,' she said, drawing out the syllables as if he were a bit slow on the uptake, which he was because he was having trouble processing what she was saying. 'So if you'll excuse me I'd better get a move on.'

Leaving him standing there like a tongue-tied brainless idiot, she turned and set off for the house at such a cracking pace she was practically through the front door by the time his brain had kicked in and he realised that she really was intending to leave and that if he wanted to stop her he was going to have to be quick.

Setting his jaw, he strode after her, dumped the roses on the table just inside the door, which was groaning with presents, and when he saw her halfway up the stairs swiftly crossed the hall. 'You're leaving now?' he said, wondering why she'd changed her mind.

'I have a train to catch,' she said without breaking stride. 'In just under an hour.'

'You weren't planning to stay?'

'No.'

'Why not?'

'Because I knew this wouldn't be the kind of wedding that goes on till dawn and I have to be at work early tomorrow.'

'Tomorrow's Sunday.'

'So?'

Taking the stairs two at a time, he caught up with her in a matter of seconds. Long enough for it to get into his thick skull that she had no intention of changing her plans despite what had happened earlier. Which disappointed him more than it ought to, although he didn't have time to wonder about that right now.

At the top of the stairs he gripped her wrist and she stilled, but he could feel her pulse racing beneath his fingers, which he didn't think was hammering just from the exertion of climbing the stairs. 'What's going on, Celia?'

'Nothing's going on,' she said flatly, tugging her hand away and rubbing her wrist. 'I just have to get back, that's all. I really do.'

He believed her because her dedication to her work was something only an hour or so ago he'd been admiring. Now, though, it just pissed him off because basically she was

LUCY KING 75

letting him know in no uncertain terms that, regardless of the attraction that still existed between them, continuing where they'd left off was at the bottom of her list of priorities. While it was at the top of his.

'You know, you really need to address that work-life balance of yours,' he drawled, oddly hurt by the idea she attached so little importance to it.

'To make it more like yours, you mean?' she said, marching across the landing towards a bedroom.

He followed her through the door and leaned back against a wall as he watched her pick up a suitcase, drop it on the bed and fling the top back. 'Working on a Sunday isn't normal.'

'It is if you have a tricky deal that needs to be pushed through in record time. Not to mention a document that's gone missing and of which I have the only copy.' She scooped up a handful of clothes, dumped them beside the suitcase and began folding and packing, folding and packing, still looking everywhere but at him. 'I wouldn't expect you to understand, what with you now being a man of leisure.'

The mocking judgemental tone that he'd assumed had gone was back, and it annoyed him even more. 'I've put in my fair share of weekends at work.'

'At the moment I work *every* weekend,' she said pointedly, and he found himself frowning and wondering, what the hell was this? Some kind of competition? 'Taking today off was a luxury,' she added, 'and I need to make it up.'

'What about what happened this afternoon?'

'What about it?' She paused in the folding/packing thing she had going on and stared at him as if she didn't have a clue what he was getting at. Which wasn't entirely surprising since he wasn't sure *he* had a clue what he was getting at. So she didn't want to spend the night with him. What was the big deal? Why was he pursuing it? And, actually, wasn't he beginning to sound a bit pathetic? A bit needy? A bit desperate?

He was, so he bit back the urge to ask her if the afternoon had meant anything to her, because it clearly hadn't, and stamped out the disappointment swirling around inside him.

'Forget it,' he said, fixing a cool smile to his face and reminding himself that it hadn't meant anything to him either. It had been good sex, nothing more, and it wasn't as if he'd never had good sex before.

She sighed and stopped folding. 'Look, Marcus, this afternoon was fun but we both know it wouldn't have gone anywhere.'

Did they? He'd thought that they'd been about to go back to his hotel room, and had hoped that things might carry on when they got back to London, but clearly he'd been picking up the wrong signals. No matter. 'I know it wouldn't have gone anywhere,' he said, and she was right. Ultimately it wouldn't.

'Yet you're sounding like you thought this was more than it was.'

He had. Maybe. A bit. For a moment. 'Evidently my mistake.'

'It's unlike you to make a mistake about something like this.'

It was. Which was undoubtedly why he was feeling so wrong-footed. The thing making his stomach churn was confusion at the unexpected turn of events, that was all. 'I blame the champagne.'

'Did I ever agree to leave with you?'

No, dammit, she hadn't, he realised belatedly. He'd jumped to that conclusion all by himself and he'd been an idiot to do so. 'No.'

'So that's it, then,' she said as if there was nothing more to be said. 'Just think of me as another of your conquests.'

'I'll do that.'

'But it was fun.'

'It was.'

'And *so* what I needed,' she said with a smile, looking at him *finally,* 'so thank you for letting me use you.'

Her words sank in and for a moment Marcus didn't know what to say. For the first time in years, he was speechless, because of all the things that he'd thought about since they'd had sex it had never once occurred to him that she'd used him.

If he'd contemplated her motives he'd have come up with something pretty much along the same lines as his. Overwhelming desire. Years of pent-up build-up. Irresistibility. An interest in seeing where things might go. He'd never have guessed that all she was after was a one-night stand. And didn't that make him a fool because he'd told her that he and the women he slept with were always on the same page, yet here he was, not just on another page but in a different book entirely.

So much for the idea that Celia was vulnerable, he thought, feeling something inside him that had momentarily thawed ice over again. So much for the thought she needed protecting. She was made of steel. She had no soft centre. And he'd been a complete and utter idiot to imagine otherwise, because he might be many things but he didn't use people, whereas she had absolutely no qualms about doing such a thing.

'No problem at all,' he said, pushing himself off the wall and making for the door, wiping Celia and the afternoon from his head with the kind of ruthless determination that had got him back on track and made him a millionaire at twenty-five. 'Happy to have helped. Have a good journey home and I'll see you around.'

CHAPTER SIX

OVER THE NEXT month Celia was so flat out at work that Marcus barely crossed her mind. She had a deal to think about. Contracts. Documents. Emails and calls and meetings and an ever overflowing in tray. She didn't have the mental space or the time to think about that afternoon. Except in the early hours of the morning when she did make it to bed and couldn't sleep, of course. Then, dizzy with exhaustion, she let herself remember and indulge, knowing that come daybreak the memory would be buried beneath work, work and more work.

Despite his parting shot, she hadn't seen him around. She hadn't expected to. For one thing, Dan—their only real reason for coming across each other—was still on honeymoon, and for another, why on earth would Marcus choose to put himself in her path after she'd deliberately told him that she'd used him?

She pushed open the door of the bar and cringed as the memory of the scene that had taken place in Zoe's parents' spare room flashed into her head.

It hadn't been her finest moment, she had to admit. In fact it had been one of her lowest, but she hadn't known what else to do. She'd had to get him out of that room before she'd run out of clothes to fold and pack and no longer had anything to distract her from the knowledge that they were in far too close proximity to a bed and she wanted him badly, despite being well aware that he was the last person she should want.

What had happened in the kitchen garden was meant to have been a blip. The release of fifteen years' worth of build-up, and closure. But as she'd stood in that driveway waving Dan and Zoe off, a sudden wave of longing for what they had had rushed over her and had thrown her even more off balance.

Totally bewildered by what was going on inside her head, she'd just wanted to escape. So she'd headed into the house, fleeing the romance and sentimentality of the afternoon, the happy, mildly boozed-up guests, the sinking sun, the sky streaked with red and the lengthening shadows, ready to pack up and leave and figure things out in the cool peace of her flat.

Marcus had followed her, of course he had. Naturally enough, given that she hadn't given him cause to think otherwise, he'd assumed that she was intending to leave with him. And for a split second she'd been so very tempted to do just that. Logically she knew that he'd never be the man for her, but that hadn't stopped her for one crazy moment desperately wanting him to be. And it had scared the living daylights out of her, which was why she'd pushed him away.

Not that she generally thought about it much. She'd analysed it to death on the train home, staring blankly out of the window as the countryside rushed by, her laptop remaining closed on the table in front of her. Once she'd got home, satisfied she'd done the right thing by putting a stop to anything more, she'd cast it from her mind.

But as she was about to have a quick drink with Lily—who hadn't taken no for an answer—Marcus and what they'd got up to the afternoon of the wedding had snuck into her head quite a bit today. And every time she did find herself losing herself in the memory she went all soft and warm inside. It was infuriating, not least because she had plenty of other more important things to think about and really didn't need the distraction.

Spying Lily sitting at a table in the corner of the busy City wine bar and fiddling with her phone, Celia weaved through the tightly packed clientele and wondered if it was overly hot in here or if it was just her.

'Hi,' she said, eventually making it over, then shrugging out of her jacket, draping it over the back of the chair and sitting down.

'Hello,' said Lily, putting her phone on the table and glancing up with a broad beam. That faded as swiftly as her eyes widened. 'God, you look dreadful.'

Celia bristled even though Lily was right. She was looking awful at the moment, which was why she tried to avoid the mirror as much as she could because she knew her skin was pasty, her eyes were puffy and her body several pounds lighter than it should be, and who needed visual proof of that? 'Thanks.'

'Well, sorry, but you do.' Lily filled a glass with wine and pushed it towards her. 'Here. You look like you could do with this.'

'Thanks,' she said again.

'So what is it?'

Celia shrugged and took a sip. 'Just work,' she said, her stomach shrivelling a little at the acidity. 'Things are pretty hectic at the moment,' she added, although in reality 'pretty hectic' didn't come close to describing her workload at the moment.

Lily frowned. 'Are you all right?'

'Oh, I'm fine,' she said, pasting a smile to her face and making an effort to relax. 'It's just a phase. This stage is always like this. And it's not like I'm the only one putting in the hours. We all are.'

Lily sat back and twiddled the stem of her glass between her fingers as she looked at her thoughtfully. 'Don't you ever worry about burning out?'

'All the time,' she said with a smile that was wry because

in reality there was no way in hell she was burning out. She couldn't afford the time.

Still, she could definitely do with maybe a bit more sleep because she was exhausted, these headaches were a pain, and the heart palpitations that had started last week were beginning to get a bit more frequent and a bit longer in duration.

If she was being honest she hadn't been feeling all that great for a while. Maybe she'd make an appointment with her GP, although she knew he'd simply tell her that it was stress and she should ease up on work. As if it were that simple.

Or maybe tonight she'd try and get home early, although given it was already nine and the bottle of wine on the table was full that seemed unlikely. In fact, seeing as she was going to be here for a while she might as well head back to the office once she was done here, do a bit more work and then spend the night there.

But it was fine. She'd survive. She always had in the past. Anyway, the deal was nearly done and then she'd catch up. On sleep. With friends. On everything else that had been put on hold.

'So what's news?' she said, taking another sip of wine and assuring herself that she and her manic schedule could easily stick it out for another week or so.

'Nothing in particular. Busy at work.'

'Missing Zoe?' she asked, thinking that as Zoe was responsible for half of the sisters' business her absence must be making things tough.

'Heaps. But it's fine. I'm managing. Are you missing Dan?'

'A bit.'

Her brother had never been away for two months before and she regularly found herself picking up the phone to call him, putting it down a second later and feeling rather empty and alone. It didn't help that her parents had been in regular touch to have a moan about each other. Usually she shared the brunt of their non-relationship with Dan, and the fact that she couldn't only added to her current stress levels.

'Kit and I have set a date for the wedding,' said Lily, dragging her out of one pity party and tossing her into another.

A wedding, Celia thought, her heart squeezing for a moment. Another one… Then she pulled herself together and remembered that once the deal was through, rectifying her love life was something else she was going to tackle. The minute she had the time she'd embark on a dating mission to end all dating missions. And because this was Lily and she was aware of the ups and downs of her and Kit's relationship, she was genuinely pleased they'd set a date. 'When?'

'December.'

'Congratulations.'

'Thanks.'

'How are things going with you two?'

'Remarkably well,' said Lily, looking a bit surprised at the thought. 'But let's not forget that there's every possibility I'll muck it up.'

Celia smiled. 'I'd be surprised if Kit let you.'

'He keeps telling me he won't.'

'There you go, then.'

'And speaking of gorgeous men,' Lily continued. 'I ran into Marcus last week.'

At the casual mention of his name Celia felt her heart lurch and her hand shake, and she put her glass on the table. 'Really?' she said, her throat dry and scratchy as she thought that, damn, stress had a lot to answer for.

Lily nodded. 'At a party.'

'Where else?'

'Want to know how he is?'

A surge of curiosity rose up inside her but she stamped

it down hard because she couldn't care less. 'Why would I want to know how he is?'

'Well, you know, after what happened at Dan and Zoe's wedding.'

Celia felt her entire body flush and this time she knew it had nothing to do with an overheated bar. 'Nothing happened.'

'Not what it looked like when I interrupted you.'

'We'd been chatting, that's all.'

'So you said. And I believe you as much now as I did then.' Lily drained her glass. 'You know, I don't blame you in the slightest. Marcus is seriously hot.'

So was she. Boiling. 'Aren't you supposed to be getting married in December?' she said a bit tetchily.

Lily grinned. 'Doesn't stop me from appreciating a fine specimen of manhood when I see one.'

Marcus wasn't a fine specimen of manhood. Yes, he was gorgeous, and he'd helped her out when she'd asked for it, but he was still as promiscuous as he'd ever been.

On the *extremely* rare occasion he'd crossed her mind in the week that followed the wedding when, despite her best efforts, the freshness of it all had meant that it refused to scuttle to the back of her mind where she wanted it, she'd found herself wondering if she hadn't made a mistake in pushing him away. Something about the look in his eye when she'd finally plucked up the guts to look at him back there in that bedroom made her wonder if maybe he'd been disappointed that she hadn't wanted to stay. If maybe he'd hoped for something more. If maybe she'd misjudged him yet again.

But she hadn't and he clearly hadn't wanted anything more because, why, only last week he'd been snapped outside some theatre or other with not just one, but two blondes hanging off his arms. The week before that he'd escorted a ravishing brunette to some charity gala in aid of cancer research. And the week before that he'd been on a beach in the Mediterranean cavorting in the waves with a bevy of Sardinian beauties.

Not that she'd been checking up on him or anything, but what was he doing about those projects he'd told her about while all this partying was going on? No mention of *them* in any of the papers.

'Well, whatever,' she said with a nonchalant shrug. 'I have no idea where Marcus is or what he's doing and I really don't care.'

'OK, you win,' said Lily with a smile and a dismissive wave of her hand that had she been firing on all cylinders Celia would have found suspicious. 'Want to come for supper next Saturday?'

As she wasn't firing on all cylinders Celia relaxed and thought that yes, she did. Very much. And not just because she was thankful for the change of subject. The deadline for the deal was next Friday so Saturday would be her first day off in weeks. She had no plans other than to sleep, so supper at Lily's after a twenty-four-hour nap sounded like a fine way to celebrate. There'd be good food, plenty of fabulous wine and possibly even a gorgeous single man or two for her to set her sights on.

'That would be lovely,' she said, with genuine gratitude. 'Thank you.'

Lily beamed and refilled their glasses. 'Great. Now let me tell you all about my wedding plans so far.'

What the hell he was doing standing on Kit and Lily's doorstep and ringing the bell Marcus had no idea.

By now he ought to have picked Melissa up and taken her to the opening night of an exhibition one of his artist friends was putting on. He ought to be sipping champagne, discussing perspective and admiring his date. Yet he'd ditched both Mel and the exhibition in order to be here.

Why he'd changed the habit of a lifetime and wilfully cancelled one plan for another he didn't want to consider too closely. He had the horrible suspicion that if he did he'd find it had quite a lot to do with Lily's mention in passing that Celia was also on the guest list, and frankly that didn't make any sense at all because Celia had made it perfectly clear that she didn't want to have anything to do with him any more and he'd taken that on board. He was totally fine with it. Hadn't thought about it for a second more, once he'd got back to London that Sunday morning.

It wasn't as if he'd been sitting at home burning with disappointment that she'd rebuffed him again, moping around like a wet weekend and feeling sorry for himself. He'd had a great time in the past month. He'd hit the social scene with a fervour bordering on vengeance. He'd dated a string of intelligent, entertaining, beautiful women, although irritatingly enough none of them had made him want to go further than a friendly goodnight kiss, let alone scratch beneath the surface. He'd taken a week's holiday just because he hadn't had one in years and now he could. And in amongst the fun he'd slowly been making plans about what he wanted to do next work-wise.

All in all he'd barely had a moment to himself, and he'd congratulated himself on not having thought about Celia once.

Yet when Lily had rung him up a week or so ago inviting him to dinner and mentioning Celia was coming, for some unfathomable reason his pulse had started thumping in a way it hadn't since that afternoon in the walled garden and he'd found himself mentally ditching his plans and saying yes, even though he didn't know either Lily or Kit all that well.

So there was little point in pretending that Celia didn't have anything to do with the reason he was here and even less point in continuing to tell himself that because he thought about her at night instead of during the day it didn't count.

In all honesty it was unsettling just how much she *did* invade his thoughts during the hours of darkness. The minute he crashed into bed she was right there with him, messing with his sleep by filling his dreams and doing the kinds of things to him that had him frequently jerking awake, hot and hard and shuddering with desire.

Which meant he probably shouldn't be here, he thought, a film of sweat breaking out all over his body, because what was he expecting? That she'd be as happy to see him as he suspected he would be to see her? What was he? A masochist?

Celia wouldn't be pleased to see him any more now than she'd been to have him following her into Zoe's parents' house that sunny Saturday afternoon. No doubt she'd be making her displeasure known the instant he walked in and be reverting to acerbity at the earliest available opportunity.

Frankly he didn't think he had the stomach for it any more, not now he knew how it could be between them.

But it was too late to back out now because even as his head churned with the desire to leave he heard the sounds of a catch being turned. The door swung open and there was Lily smiling broadly and waving him in, and he had no option but to grit his teeth and brace himself to get through the next couple of hours the best he could.

'Marcus,' she said warmly, 'I'm so glad you could make it. Come in.'

'Thanks.' He stepped over the threshold and handed over the bottle and the box, and smiled as she let out a little whoop. 'Champagne and truffles,' she said, grinning even more widely. 'A perfect combination. Thank you. Come and meet everyone.'

He followed her down the hall, listening for one voice, one laugh, every cell of his body on high alert. More tense than he'd been at any point over the past month, he walked into the sitting room, the smile on his face still firmly in place. He shook hands with Kit and accepted a gin and tonic. Then he nodded and chatted as he was introduced to their friends, all the while scouring the room for Celia.

Who wasn't there.

Late? he wondered, or—

'She couldn't make it,' murmured Lily, who'd clearly been watching him scan the guests.

'Who couldn't?' he said, annoyed at both wanting to see her and at being so transparent.

She rolled her eyes. 'Celia.'

'Shame,' he said coolly, and knocked back a slug of his drink.

'Yes. A headache apparently.'

Perhaps brought on by the discovery that he'd also been invited? He didn't know whether to be thrilled, cheated or devastated that she wasn't going to be there. 'So nothing serious, then.'

'Only for my table plan,' said Lily with a grin, before sobering. 'Actually, she didn't sound too good at all.'

'Oh?'

'In fact, she sounded dreadful.'

Marcus kept his face expressionless, and ignored the stab of concern that struck him squarely in the gut. Celia would be fine. A headache was nothing to someone like her. She had the constitution of an ox, a backbone of steel and ice running through her veins. 'I'm sorry to hear that,' he said evenly.

'I saw her ten days ago, you know.'

'Did you?'

'She wasn't looking well then.'

'What's the matter with her?' he asked, purely for the sake of conversation and not out of any interest whatsoever.

'I'm not sure. It sounds like she's working hard.'

'She does that.'

'Too hard maybe.'

'She does that too.' Especially on Sundays.

'Maybe you should go and check on her.'

He went still, his hand tightening around his glass. 'Why would I want to go and check on her?' he said, the need to do just that now suddenly—and perversely—thundering through him.

'You're itching to,' said Lily, and he stamped it down because he wasn't interested in how she was, and in any case he was pretty sure that the last thing she'd want was him pitching up on her doorstep, even if she hadn't been unwell.

'No, I'm not,' he said coolly. 'How hard Celia works is entirely up to her. I couldn't care less how she is or what she's up to.'

Lily looked at him shrewdly. 'Funny, she said that about you too.'

'Did she?'

'Strikes me that there's a lot of protesting going on here.' She pretended to consider for a moment then said, 'Maybe a bit too much.'

Just about resisting the temptation to grind his teeth, Marcus had had enough of beating around this particular bush. If it went on any longer she'd crush him to dust. 'If you have a point, Lily,' he said tightly, 'would you mind getting to it?'

'My point is that you get to each other.'

'And?'

'You should do something about it.'

He'd tried. He'd failed. He wouldn't be going there again. Or even thinking about it. 'She knows where I am.'

Lily let out a huff of exasperation. 'Oh, for heaven's sake, will you just go and see if she's all right? As a favour to me? Please.'

At the genuine worry now filling Lily's eyes, Marcus felt

his resolve begin to waver and silently cursed. Oh, bloody hell. What choice did he have? He might not be keen to see her but if Celia was in real trouble, as Lily clearly thought she was, would he ever be able to forgive himself if he'd had the chance to help her and had done nothing, simply out of dented pride? Would Dan? And if she wasn't in trouble, well, surely he could deal with the tongue-lashing he'd undoubtedly get.

Sighing deeply, he ran a hand across the back of his neck. 'OK, fine,' he said, and then, because he'd never be able to sit through supper, chatting and laughing while the visit to Celia's loomed, added, 'Want me to go now?'

Lily beamed. 'I think it would be best, don't you? And actually, as it would even up my table plan you'd be doing me a favour. Another one,' she added, ushering him back down the hall and opening the door he'd stepped through only ten minutes before.

'Text me her address and apologise to Kit for me.'

She nodded. 'I will. Give her my love and tell her I said to get well soon. And thank you, Marcus.'

'No problem,' he said, and with the vague suspicion that, for all his reputation, when it came to powers of persuasion he had nothing on Lily, he left.

CHAPTER SEVEN

HALF AN HOUR later Marcus had crossed London and was at the top of the steps that led up to Celia's building, thinking that here he was unexpectedly standing on yet another doorstep he'd had no intention of gracing a week ago.

As the taxi had pulled up at her address he'd noticed that her lights were off and for a split second he'd contemplated leaving her be. But then Lily and Dan had shot into his thoughts, and his conscience—which had never given him much trouble before—had sprung into life, propelling him out of the taxi and up the steps.

So he'd do what he was here to do. He'd check on her, and then go, and with any luck he wouldn't have any reason to see her ever again, bar the odd Dan/Zoe occasion that might require both their presence.

Marginally reassured by that, he pressed the buzzer and waited. He shoved his hands in his pockets and rocked on his heels for a couple of minutes. Was just about to give up when the intercom crackled to life.

'Yes?' came the muffled voice.

'Celia,' he said, leaning forwards. 'It's Marcus.'

There was silence. And then a grumpy, 'What the hell are you doing here?'

Yup, as he'd thought. No more pleased to have him visit than he was. 'To see if you're all right.'

'Why wouldn't I be?'

'You tell me. I heard you had a headache.'

'I do. I was asleep.'

'Then I apologise for waking you up.'

'Not accepted,' she said crossly. There was a rustle, and then, 'Wait. How did you hear about my headache?'

'Dinner. Kit and Lily's. You were meant to be there.'

A pause while she presumably processed this fact. 'That's right,' she said slowly, as if realisation had only just dawned. 'I was. Have I missed it?'

'Half of it at least.'

'How rude of me.'

'Not *that* rude. You cancelled.'

'Did I?'

OK, so this was getting a little odd, thought Marcus with a frown as a flicker of concern edged through his frustration. Celia sounded confused, disorientated. Which was possibly a consequence of being abruptly woken up. Or possibly not. 'Apparently so.'

'Oh,' she said vaguely. 'So why aren't you still there?'

'Lily was worried.'

'She has no need to be. I'm fine.'

At the ensuing silence he sighed and ran a hand through his hair and wished to God that her brother were here. Even either of her parents—who both unfortunately lived a couple of hundred miles away—would do because he was *not* the man for this job. However, something was telling him she wasn't all that fine, and right now there was no one else. 'Can I come up? Just for a second.'

'I'm not a child, Marcus,' she said, frustration clear in her voice. 'I don't need checking up on or looking after.'

'Then prove it and let me in. Five minutes. That's all I ask.'

There was a pause. A sigh. 'Then will you leave me alone?'

'Yes.' If she really was as all right as she claimed.

'OK, fine.'

The door buzzed and Marcus pushed it open. He leapt up the four flights of stairs to Celia's top-floor flat, and at the sight of her he stopped dead, the breath knocked from his lungs.

She was standing in the doorway, her arms crossed and her chin up, and she might be channelling defiance and trying to appear all right, but she looked absolutely horrendous. Her skin was grey, her eyes dull and her hair was all over the place. She was wearing a pair of faded pink pyjamas that had seen better days, and even though she was covered from head to toe he was willing to bet that she'd lost weight. Her cheeks were hollower than they'd been the last time he'd seen her and her collarbones sharper.

Apart from that ten minutes with him in the garden, she always looked immaculate. Magnificent. Totally together and composed. Now, though, she looked like a dishevelled ghost, the energy and drive all sucked out of her, and it shocked the life out of him.

Frustration gone and concern sweeping in to take its place, he strode towards her, then, as she stepped back to let him in, past her into her flat and spun round as she closed the door behind him.

'What on earth is the matter with you?' he said, worry making his voice sharper than he'd intended.

Celia winced and put a hand to her temple. 'Don't shout at me.'

Guilt slashed through him and he swore softly. 'Sorry.'

'I have a headache.'

'So you said,' he said, gritting his teeth in an effort to moderate his tone, 'but this looks like more than just a headache to me.'

'I guess it might be a migraine but I've never had one so I wouldn't know.'

'Have you taken anything for it?'

'Aspirin, but it hasn't made any difference.' She walked past him into the kitchen and picked up a bottle of water, holding it to her chest as if she needed the defence. 'You really didn't need to come over,' she grumbled. 'I'm sure I'll be fine in the morning.'

'Possibly.'

'I'm just tired, that's all.'

He glanced at the dark circles beneath her eyes and thought that exhausted was more like it. And she was way too thin. 'When did you last eat?'

She frowned then shrugged. 'Yesterday evening. The deal went through and we went out to celebrate.'

'Congratulations.'

'Thanks.'

'I'll make you something and then put you to bed.'

She jerked, her eyes widening and her cheeks flushing, which at least gave her some colour. 'No,' she said hotly. 'Absolutely not.'

At the thought evidently going through her mind Marcus let out a sigh of exasperation and dragged a hand through his hair. 'Oh, for heaven's sake, Celia.'

Her eyes flashed. 'I *don't* need a nurse.'

'You need food.'

'I need to be left alone.'

'Well, that's too bad because I'm not going anywhere.' Two could play the obstinacy game, and with the state she was in she didn't stand a chance of winning. How on earth could he leave her when she obviously wasn't well at all? Dan would have his balls on a plate.

'I hate you seeing me like this,' she said.

He hated seeing her like this too. He'd always thought of her as so strong and resilient, and to see her a mere shadow of herself was twisting something in his chest. 'I've no doubt you do, but you might as well get used to it.'

'Well, you can't make me something to eat,' she said, clearly sensing that this battle was one she wasn't going to win and, to his relief, giving in. 'There's nothing in the fridge apart from bread. I don't cook, remember.'

'Then we'll get something in.'

'Not sure I feel like eating.'

Ignoring that, Marcus spied the pile of takeaway menus on the immaculately gleaming counter, snatched up the one on the top and hauled out his phone. Tonight, it seemed, they'd be having pizza. Not quite the gourmet spread Lily had probably planned, but good enough.

'What else is wrong besides the headache?' he asked, tapping the number into his phone.

'Nothing, really.'

He shot her a look of warning. 'Celia.'

'OK, sometimes I ache.'

'Ache where?'

'All over.'

'And?'

She bit her lip and frowned. 'I might have been having a few heart palpitations as well.'

Marcus froze, then blanched, his thumb hovering over the dial button. Migraines? Aches? Heart palpitations? What the hell was wrong with her? 'A few?'

She shrugged. 'More than a few.'

'Anything else?'

'No, that's about it, I think.'

Well, it was quite enough, he thought grimly, deleting the number and scrolling through his list of contacts. Sod the pizza. Sod tucking her up in bed and keeping an eye on her till morning. She was going to see a doctor. Now.

'I need a taxi,' he said the second his call was answered, and then reeled off her address.

'I thought you were calling for food,' she said, looking a bit bewildered.

'Change of plan.' Then into the phone, 'No. Half an hour's too long. Make it ten minutes and I'll double the fare.' And with that he hung up.

'Where are you going?' she asked.

'*We* are going to A and E.'

She stared at him in surprise and then gave a weak laugh. 'I'm sure I don't need to go to A and E, Marcus. I'll just take some more aspirin and go back to bed. You're overreacting.'

He looked at her steadily. 'Heart palpitations, Celia?'

'Stress,' she said firmly, dismissively, and he wanted to shake her. 'Which will undoubtedly diminish now that the deal's gone through.'

'What if it isn't just stress?'

'What else would it be?'

'I don't know,' he said, struggling to keep a lid on his temper because she just didn't seem to be taking this seriously and it was threatening to make him lose it. 'How about burnout? How about a breakdown? How about a bloody heart attack?'

She recoiled. Went as white as the walls of her pristine flat, and he bit back an instinctive apology because he was glad he'd shocked her. She *should* be concerned.

'Fine,' she said, coolly rallying and pulling her shoulders back. 'You win. I'll go and get dressed, then, shall I?'

By the time Celia's name was called four hours later and she went off to see the doctor Marcus was practically climbing walls.

She'd been quiet while they'd been waiting. Monosyllabic in her answers to his occasional question about how she was feeling, but that was hardly surprising since he must have put the fear of God into her with talk of burnout, breakdown and heart attacks. Not to mention the way he'd practically bullied her into coming, even though he'd had no choice because, God, he'd never met a more stubborn woman.

But she hadn't commented on his methods or his motivation, which was actually something of a relief because he wasn't sure he could explain the reason for the sky-high level of concern that had gripped him when he'd laid eyes on her earlier. He could tell himself as much as he liked that it was Lily, or Dan, or his conscience, but he had the vague suspicion it was something else. Something he didn't want to investigate too closely.

Instead she'd just sat there, calmly flicking through leaflets and then absorbing herself in her e-reader. She'd drunk the coffees he'd bought, and worked her way through half a sandwich, an apple and a chocolate bar that he'd picked up from the canteen. She'd even had a nap, stretching across four of the uncomfortable plastic chairs and point-blank refusing the offer of his lap as a pillow.

In short, she couldn't have been more composed.

He, on the other hand, had been going increasingly nuts. When not occupied with the job of going for food and drink, he'd spent practically all of the past four hours pacing, shoving his hands through his hair in frustration and wishing he could just barge in and insist she be seen then and there. But this was a Saturday night in London, and a woman with a headache and the odd palpitation—as she'd insisted on describing herself when asked about her symptoms—came pretty low down on the list when it came to emergencies.

He didn't like hospitals; the smells, the lighting, the sounds made him shudder. He'd spent quite enough time in them when his father had been ill. He didn't like the memories they stirred up much either. Memories of his mother's grief following his father's death and the way she'd shut him out. The way he hadn't understood that and so had reciprocated by shutting her—and everyone else—out.

As an only child with an emotionally absent mother he'd been alone with his grief, and, unable to handle it, he'd gone off the rails, partying too hard, drinking too much and sleeping with too many girls. He hadn't noticed that his mother wasn't coping either. She hadn't displayed any sign that she wasn't and he hadn't realised she'd been caught in the claws of deep depression until the day he learned she'd locked herself in the garage with the engine of his father's car running and had had to identify her body in yet another hospital.

But where else could he have taken Celia at this time on a Saturday night? It was the only option he'd had because maybe she was right and he was overreacting but the symptoms she had worried him, and if it came to it he was not going to have another woman's death on his conscience.

Given that they'd been waiting so long, the fact that Celia emerged a mere fifteen minutes after she went in was unexpected. He didn't know if the speed of her appointment was a good thing or a bad one. He scoured her face but her expression gave nothing away. She didn't look happy. Or sad. She just looked blank.

As she went and sat down, Marcus strode over to her, his heart pounding and his blood draining to his feet as something like dread began to sweep through him. God, if there was something really wrong with her he didn't know what the hell he'd do.

'What is it?' he asked.

She looked up at him. Blinked as if whatever the doctor had told her hadn't sunk in yet, and he got the impression that she wasn't really looking at him. That she was miles away.

'Celia? Tell me. What is it?'

She opened her mouth. Closed it. Frowned. 'Stress, mainly,' she said finally.

Marcus sank into the chair next to her, almost sagging with relief. Not a breakdown. Not burnout. Not a heart attack. 'Thank God for that,' he said roughly.

'I wouldn't go thanking God just yet.'

'Why not?'

'Because it's not just stress.'

'Then what else is it?'

'I'm pregnant.'

* * *

Celia watched as the news she'd barely registered herself hit Marcus' brain. Watched him reel as she was still reeling. Watched the shock cross his face and thought that it couldn't be anywhere near as great as the shock she was feeling. The shock that had made her throw up in the doctor's wastepaper basket, not that she'd be sharing that delightful detail with him.

'Pregnant?' he echoed faintly.

She nodded. 'Six weeks, they think.'

'Mine?'

'Couldn't be anyone else's.'

Marcus swore brutally and shoved his hands through his hair.

'I know,' she muttered.

Except she didn't really know anything about anything that had happened in the past six or so hours. She didn't know why when Marcus had rung her buzzer she'd wanted him to leave, not because she'd thought she was fine, but because she hadn't wanted him to see her in such a state. She didn't know why she'd secretly been so pleased that he'd refused to take her hints and go. Why she was glad he'd insisted on her coming to A and E. Why she was grateful for his support now.

She was a modern, intelligent, self-sufficient woman. She shouldn't need looking after. She shouldn't like it. It didn't make any sense. But then nothing about her behaviour around Marcus made much sense. Her reaction to him after a month of not seeing him certainly didn't. He ought to have no effect on her at all, because she was so over him and what they'd done, yet he'd mentioned tucking her up in bed—platonically, obviously—and she'd nearly gone up in flames. He'd suggested she rest her head in his lap and she'd practically scooted over to a row of seats on the other side of the waiting room.

Despite the composed front she'd put on she'd been almost unbearably tense. And not just because of the effect
Marcus had on her. Deep down the way she'd been feeling
for the past couple of weeks had terrified her. Not that what
she'd found out once she'd been called to see the doctor had
dispelled any of the tension.

She'd gone in there imagining that maybe she'd be told
to ease up on work. Perhaps be prescribed the beta block-
ers that most of her colleagues seemed to be on.

The appointment had started normally enough. The doctor had taken a note of her symptoms. He'd asked her about
work and then her menstrual cycle. When she hadn't been
able to tell him the date of her last period he'd asked her
whether she'd had sex recently.

And then it turned a bit chilling. The questions began to
head in one horrible direction, terminating with her pee-
ing on a white plastic stick and two blue lines appearing.

What had come after that was a bit of a blur. All she'd
been able to hear was a sort of rushing in her ears through
which the doctor's warning about the dangers of stress and
the instruction to make an appointment with her GP had
only very dimly filtered. Then she'd stumbled out on legs
that felt weak and wobbly and wholly unfit for purpose, and
collapsed into the nearest chair.

'What the hell happened?'

At the sound of Marcus' voice, shock and horror evident
in every word, Celia snapped to and blinked. 'Condoms are
only ninety-eight per cent safe,' she said, recalling the sta-
tistic she'd read in one of the leaflets she'd flicked through
earlier and what the doctor had reiterated. 'Seems like we're
one of the unlucky two per cent.'

'How?'

'I don't know. Maybe it had expired. Maybe it wasn't on
properly. Maybe it broke. Who knows?'

As they lapsed into silence she could hear the plasticky

tick of the clock on the wall, the hum of a busy hospital A and E department and the distant chatter of staff, but the sounds of the cogs and wheels of her brain were fast taking over and her head was beginning to ache more than it had at any point today.

'So what the hell do we do now?' he said, still sounding a bit stunned.

'I have absolutely no idea.' And now, with all the adrenaline draining away and events catching up with her, she suddenly felt very, very tired. 'And you know what, Marcus?' she said, getting to her feet and hauling the strap of her handbag over her shoulder. 'It's late, I'm shattered and I don't think I can deal with this right now.'

He glanced up at her, frowned as he scanned her face, and then stood. 'I'll take you home.'

'I'd appreciate that,' she said with a weak smile. And then, just in case he got it into his head that he'd be staying and fussing over her when she wanted nothing more than to sleep and then process the news and figure out what she wanted to do about it in her own time, added, 'But then, if you don't mind, I'd like to be alone.'

Marcus did mind. Very much. Still. Even though he'd got home a couple of hours ago and Celia probably hadn't given him a moment's thought the second he'd driven away.

He hadn't wanted to leave her. He'd wanted to stay the night. He'd wanted to put her to bed and then keep an eye on her to make sure she was all right because she'd had quite a shock and in her fragile state he wasn't sure how she'd cope with it.

But she'd thanked him for dropping her off, told him she'd call when she was ready to talk and said a very firm goodnight. And now he was at home, sitting in his study, staring out into the garden and working his way through the bottle of whisky that had been gathering dust unopened at the back of a cupboard in the kitchen.

Thinking.

Remembering.

Wondering.

And, the more he thought about that afternoon, going into such mental detail that he could recall every move they'd made, finally realising what had probably happened.

Celia had been wrong in only two of her answers to his stunned enquiry into how she'd got pregnant. The condom hadn't expired. And he had enough experience to be able to put it on properly, however desperate he was.

But he *had* ripped at the packet with his teeth.

He could see it now. His body shaking. His hands trembling as he fumbled for the condom and he bit at it, his teeth very likely nipping a hole in the latex...

He swore again and shoved his hands through his hair. How the hell had he made such a schoolboy error? He'd *never* been so heavy-handed. So damn careless. What was it about Celia that had made him lose his mind so completely that for the first time in his life he'd screwed up? And how the hell hadn't he noticed something was amiss afterwards?

Her pregnancy was his fault, he thought grimly, refilling the glass for perhaps the sixth time although he'd stopped counting at three. Entirely his fault. She'd just had her life turned upside down because of him and his complete and utter loss of control and there was no one to blame but him.

Which meant that what happened next wasn't up to him. Back in the hospital he'd asked what the hell they did now, but there was no 'they' about this. It was up to her. Wholly up to her.

How he did or didn't feel about fatherhood—and he couldn't allow himself to think about it—was irrelevant. He didn't have the right to form an opinion about it either way. Whatever course of action she chose she was the one who'd have to physically go through it. He'd put her in a position he was pretty sure she'd never expected to find herself in, so all he could do was accept whatever choice she made and offer his support.

The best thing he could do *now,* he thought, screwing the lid on the bottle and taking it and his glass through to the kitchen—the only thing he could do, in fact, if he didn't want to drive himself insane with speculation and impatience—would be to put it from his mind until she was ready to talk.

CHAPTER EIGHT

PREGNANT.

Hmm.

The following morning, after what had—strangely enough, given the events of the past twelve hours—been the best night's sleep she'd had in weeks, Celia sat at the little square table in her kitchen and stared at the pile of pregnancy tests she'd bought just in case the one last night had been as faulty as the condom they'd used.

As proven by the half a dozen pairs of blue lines dancing in front of her eyes it hadn't, and so now she was going to have to face facts.

Heaven only knew how, but overnight she'd managed to block it out. Most probably she'd been in too great a state of shock, too overwhelmed by the enormity of the news and too knackered to process it. This morning, however, she felt refreshed. A bit calmer, at least with regards to her health. Her headache had gone, and the pain and palpitations were dwindling, as if discovering the reason for them—coupled with the sheer relief she hadn't been suffering any of the things that Marcus had suggested—had alleviated them.

Not that she was feeling all that calm about the fact that she was pregnant. No. That was making her insides churn, the coffee she'd drunk earlier and the toast and marmalade she'd just rustled up rolling around in her stomach and from time to time threatening to reappear.

What a bloody mess.

The emotional side of her was livid at the situation. At

bad luck, statistics that left room for failure, and most of all with herself for not being stronger willed in that damn vegetable garden.

The rational side of her thought there was little point in being angry or trying to apportion the blame. What was done was done and she just had to deal with it. She had to put all that to one side and figure out what the hell she was going to do about it, which meant that she now had to face options she'd never expected to have. Had never wanted to have.

She could keep it. Or she could not keep it.

What a choice.

A tiny piece of her wished she didn't have to make it. That the law, society, religion or even her own moral stance on the subject dictated what she had to do and the decision would be out of her hands.

But she squashed that piece of her because she was lucky to live somewhere where she had the choice. The same somewhere that gave her the opportunity to have a career, independence, freedom of thought and speech and deed.

If she gave her options the kind of logical consideration she gave everything—with the exception of that one crazy afternoon of hot sex with Marcus bloody Black—she'd come to the right decision. She trusted in her ability to do that. She was intelligent, confident and had a whole world of information at her fingertips. She'd research. Weigh up the pros and cons and search the depths of her heart and soul, if necessary. And then she'd make up her mind, and know that whatever she chose it would be the right thing to do.

For her, at least.

What Marcus' opinion on the subject would be she had no idea. But while he was many things he wasn't a fool and she had no doubt that he'd make up his mind about how he'd like to proceed, just as she would. If their wishes

coincided, great. If they didn't... Well, she'd cross that
bridge if and when they came to it.

Ever since Celia had rung at the crack of dawn this Monday
morning, Marcus had been pacing, his nerves as frayed as
the carpet he was wearing to death. The past twenty-four
hours hadn't been easy for him, although he was under no
illusion that they'd been anywhere near as tough as Celia's.

After knocking his monster hangover on the head and up-
dating Lily on Celia's state—omitting the news of her pregnancy, naturally—he'd gone to the gym, where first he'd
ploughed up and down the pool for a good couple of hours
and after that had run for miles on the treadmill. When he'd
got home he'd tried to work. Then he'd eyed the piles of pa-
perwork on his desk and thought about filing. Ten minutes
later he'd made an omelette and stuck a film on.

But no matter how hard he'd tried to distract himself
he'd still spent every single agonisingly slow second of the
day battling the desire to ring her. She'd said she'd wanted
to be left alone and he had to respect that, but it had been
hard. So when she'd called this morning he'd nearly fallen
to his knees in gratitude because he didn't think he would
have been able to hold out much longer.

Wasn't sure how much he—or his carpet—could, because by his reckoning an hour and a half went way beyond
the 'about an hour' she'd told him she'd be.

Just as he was shooting a quick frustrated glance at the
clock on the mantelpiece and wondering if he shouldn't call
her, the peal of the doorbell burst through the house and he
stopped mid-pace, whipped round and strode to the front
door. He opened it, drew it back and at the sight of her felt
a great wave of relief rock through him.

She looked *so* much better than she had on Saturday
night. Her complexion was pink instead of grey, her eyes

bright instead of dull, and even though she was still way too thin, of course, she seemed to have her energy back.

And totally unexpectedly, the overwhelming urge to pull her into his arms and kiss the life out of her slammed into him.

He curled his fingers around the edge of the door to stop himself from reaching for her and concentrated on keeping his feet planted on the floor instead of moving towards her, because taking her into his arms and kissing her was so inappropriate given the circumstances it filled him with self-disgust.

'Good morning,' she said, smiling faintly, with any luck completely unaware of what was going through his head.

'Hi,' he said, his voice so hoarse it sounded as if he hadn't used it for months. He cleared his throat, flashed her a quick smile of his own and then stepped back. 'Come in.'

'Thanks.'

She walked past him, looking up and around, at the pictures on the walls, at the furniture in the hall. Even though he'd been intending to take her straight into the kitchen and offer her a drink, when she veered into the sitting room he let her because something deep inside him, something he wasn't keen on analysing too closely, wanted her to like what she saw.

He thrust his hands into the pockets of his jeans, watched as she peered at photos, ran her gaze over his bookshelves and took in the furnishings, and he had to bite back the urge to ask her what she thought because he was pretty sure that she wasn't here to discuss his interior design.

'You have a nice house, Marcus,' she said, once they'd made it into the kitchen and he'd handed her the glass of water she'd requested when he'd offered her something to drink.

'You sound surprised,' he said, the gratification that she

liked it overriding the irritation that despite everything she still harboured some of the old impressions she'd had of him.

'I am a bit, I guess. It's big but somehow it feels cosy. Lived in.' She lifted the glass and took a sip. 'It's unexpected.'

'Why, what did you expect?'

She shrugged and shot him a smile. 'I don't know, really. Something more along the lines of a shag pad, I suppose.'

'You haven't seen the bedroom.'

The minute the words left his mouth he wished he could scoop them up and stuff them back in because that had sounded an awful lot like flirting, and what the hell he thought he was doing flirting with Celia, *now,* he had no idea.

She snapped her gaze to his, her eyes widening and her breath catching. 'No,' she said softly. 'I haven't.'

Marcus ignored the temptation to suggest that she go with him and check it out, and told himself to get a grip. He had to pull himself together. He really did. Before he made even more of a fool of himself.

'So how are you feeling?' he asked, folding his arms, leaning back against the granite counter and deciding that whatever it was that was affecting his ability to think straight it might be safer if he stuck to the likely reason she was here.

'Better after a couple of good nights' sleep,' she said dryly, 'but strange.'

'Strange' he could understand. He was feeling very strange indeed. A bit baffled by the way she was affecting him given the situation they were in. On edge and horribly awkward, which was a new one when it came to the things he felt around her. A new one for him generally, come to think of it. 'How's the headache?'

'Gone.'

'The palpitations?'

'Receding.'

Thank goodness for that. 'Nausea?'

'No.'

He ran his gaze over her figure, taking in the summery dress that hung off her a bit too loosely, and frowned. 'Are you eating?'

She nodded. 'I am.'

'Properly?'

'Properly. I went to the supermarket this morning and everything. Scout's honour.'

Good. 'So no work today, then?' he said, remembering it was Monday.

'I took the day off.'

'That must be a first.'

'The first in two years.' She shot him a quick wry smile. 'Stuff on my mind, you know?'

He did. On his mind too, actually, and frankly he'd had enough of skirting around the issue with small talk and edginess. 'So I imagine you're here to talk about the pregnancy.'

'I haven't been able to think about anything else for the last twenty-four hours.'

'No, well, it's kind of all-consuming, isn't it?'

'What's your take on it?'

He didn't have one. At least not until he knew what hers was. 'I'd rather hear yours.'

She tilted her head and looked at him steadily, a frown appearing on her forehead. 'Have you actually thought at all about what you think we should do?'

'Of course I have,' he said, because he *had* thought about it. Sort of. Not that he'd really come to a conclusion one way or another. What would have been the point of that when, as it wasn't his decision to make, any opinion he had would only be irrelevant?

'Because you do realise that the only way we can work through this is if we're honest.'

'I do.' And he would be honest, because he wanted what she wanted. 'Want to sit down?'

'Sure.'

She pulled out the nearest chair and sat down and he walked round the table to take a seat opposite her.

'OK. Right. Well. Here goes.' She put her glass on the table, leaned forwards to rest her elbows on the table and took a deep breath. 'As you can probably imagine *I've* given it a *lot* of thought and the way I see it we have three options. One, I keep it. Two, I have it and give it up for adoption. Or three, I have an abortion.'

Even though he could feel his heartbeat speeding up Marcus didn't move a muscle. 'Go on.'

'As far as I'm concerned option number two isn't viable. I have no moral grounds for going through the whole nine months of pregnancy only to give the baby away at the end.'

'So that leaves options one and three.'

She nodded. 'It does.'

'And which have you decided on?'

'Option number three.'

There. It was done.

Celia held her breath as she waited for Marcus' reaction to the conclusion she'd spent so many heart-wrenching hours coming to. So many thoughts going round and round in her head. So many scenarios playing out over and over again. So much turmoil churning around inside her.

She hadn't come to the decision easily. She'd never given anything more consideration. She'd applied logic, practicality and emotion, looking at it from every angle she could think of. And then she'd looked at it from what she thought might be Marcus' angle, even though she was becoming increasingly aware that he may have angles and depths she'd never considered before.

Given what she knew for certain of him, though, she'd

assumed that he'd be on board with her decision. That he wouldn't want the disruption to his life any more than she did.

But right now his face was so totally unreadable she couldn't tell what he was thinking and it was disconcerting to say the least.

'I see,' he said, his voice devoid of any emotion whatsoever. 'You want an abortion.'

'I wouldn't exactly say I *want* one, but I think it would be for the best.'

'Right.'

There was still nothing in his expression to let her know what he thought, and she felt a flutter of alarm. What if she'd been wrong in her assumption he'd think the same? What if he wasn't on board with this? What if he wanted the baby while she didn't? What would happen then?

'Look, Marcus,' she said, bracing herself for the possibility of having to negotiate or compromise or who knew what, 'while I don't rule out having children at some point in the future, the timing of this one couldn't be worse. My career is very important to me. I travel a lot. I work horrendous hours. I'm up for partnership, and after everything I've worked for I can't jeopardise that. This pregnancy was an accident and I—'

'You don't have to justify your decision, Celia,' he cut in, thankfully putting an end to her rambling, which was in danger of becoming faintly hysterical.

'Don't I?'

'No. Because I happen to agree with you.'

She blinked. Sat back. A little bit stunned and a whole lot relieved. 'You do? Really?'

He nodded. Once. 'Really.' He leaned forwards and looked at her, his gaze intense and unwavering. 'You wanted to know my take on it? Well, this is my take on it. I don't want a child either. It's not something I've ever wanted.

While the timing is neither here nor there for me I think we're both well aware I'm hardly father material. We're not in a relationship. And when it comes down to it I'm not sure we really even like each other.'

Oh. That took her aback, although she didn't really know why, because he was right. She might still be fiercely and annoyingly attracted to him but did that constitute like? She didn't think so.

'So what kind of people would we be bringing a child into that situation?' he continued.

'My thoughts exactly,' she murmured, and wondered if he'd somehow been able to read her mind because so many of his arguments were hers.

'We'd both end up miserable and God only knows what effect that would have on a child.'

'Not a good one, and I should know.'

'So that's it, then,' he said briskly. 'Decision made.'

Thank goodness for that. Celia blew out a breath she hadn't realised she'd been holding because this conversation had gone a lot more smoothly than she'd dared to hope. 'Are you sure?'

'I'm as sure as you are.'

And she was one hundred per cent sure. She'd employed every resource she had and had thought about it for so long and hard that how could she be anything but? 'I'm sure,' she said firmly, then she sat back, every single one of her muscles sagging in relief. 'You know, for a moment there I was really worried you'd want it,' she said with a faint smile.

'And have to curb my lifestyle?' he said dryly.

'Well, quite,' she said, her smile faltering for a second as it struck her that, while much of his behaviour recently had surprised her, some things were still the same. Such as his love of chasing after anything in a skirt. Or bikini, if those press reports of his antics over the past month, complete with photos, were anything to go by.

But she pushed aside whatever it was that was needling her—disapproval, most probably—because what did she care what he got up to, and instead focused on the tiny arrow of guilt that was suddenly stabbing at her conscience. 'Are we being terribly selfish?' she said, suspecting they were, but if they were at least they were in it together.

Marcus shook his head. 'I'd say we're being sensible. Realistic. Responsible.'

'That sounds more palatable.'

'It's true. You know it is.'

He was right. She did. 'I know.'

'So what happens next?' he asked after a moment.

'I'm going to take the rest of this week off.'

'Can you do that at such short notice?'

She shrugged, for the first time in her career not giving a toss what her boss would think. 'They'll just have to live with it. I nearly killed myself pushing that deal through. They can spare me for a week.'

'Are you serious?'

'Deadly.'

He shot her a quick grin that flipped her stomach. 'I'm staggered.'

'I know,' she said dryly, reminding herself that her stomach had no business flipping since he'd clearly moved on to pastures new. 'A temporary shift to my work-life balance. Who'd have thought? But seeing as how I've made an appointment to see my GP this afternoon—and presumably there'll be others—it makes sense. Having my boss wonder what's wrong with me is not something I'd want to encourage.'

'Want me to come along?'

She shook her head. 'I should be fine this afternoon,' she said and then, trying not to think too much about why she wanted or needed his support, added, 'But maybe you could come with me to the clinic or wherever I have to go.'

'Of course.'

'I'll call you with dates.'

Celia got to her feet and picked up her bag, and as Marcus walked her to the door she found herself wondering if he really was as on board with this as he claimed. There was something about his lack of emotion, the way he'd agreed with her so swiftly, that didn't feel quite right. She'd have thought he'd question her thought process a bit more, and the fact that he hadn't made her faintly uneasy.

He opened the door and she stopped. Turned to him and, dismissing the little voice inside her head questioning why she'd want to challenge him when his agreement suited her so well, said, 'Marcus?'

'What?'

'Do you really think we're doing the right thing?'

The look he gave her was firm and resolute and wiped away all her doubts, even before he nodded and said, 'Absolutely.'

CHAPTER NINE

BUT MARCUS KNEW that he'd lied. Unwittingly perhaps, but he'd lied nonetheless, because he didn't think they were doing the right thing at all.

Sitting with Celia in his kitchen and talking it through, he'd been convinced that going along with whatever she wanted was the only course of action he had any right to take.

But the conversation had clearly opened some kind of cupboard in his head into which he'd stuffed everything he'd told himself to block out because she'd left and within minutes his head had filled with everything he'd not allowed himself to think about.

As a result, thoughts had been ricocheting round his brain for the past three days, messy and jumbled, but all pointing to the conclusion that he thought they were making a mistake.

He couldn't explain it. He shouldn't want a child. His current lifestyle—which he worked hard at and enjoyed—wasn't conducive to one. His arguments for terminating the pregnancy had been extremely valid, and God knew all the reasons Celia had put forward were ones he could understand.

Then there was the indisputable fact that he didn't want to be tied to anyone, least of all someone who had a problem with the way he lived—and what greater tie was there than a child?

And finally there was the deep-rooted fear that history

would repeat itself and he wouldn't make it past his child's seventeenth birthday, and dread of the possible fallout from that.

Yet all he had to do was see a mental image of him holding his child in his arms and something inside him melted. When the mental image of Celia holding his child in her arms came to him, he melted even more. And as he wasn't someone who melted, ever, the feeling was both bewildering and alarming.

Rationally he knew that if she had the baby his life— and hers—would become horribly complicated and messy and fraught with tension. There'd be logistics to sort out, all kinds of obstacles to negotiate and endless arguments over decisions that would have to be made.

But none of that seemed to be of much importance.

Instead, whenever he thought about having an actual child he was assailed by memories of his own childhood. The love and attention his parents had lavished on him. The days out. The walks, the trips to the zoo, the beach. The holidays. The happy little unit they'd been before he'd hit adolescence and become a normal moody teenager.

Logically he was aware there must have been tough times and his childhood couldn't have been hearts and flowers every second, but all his memory chose to focus on were the happy ones.

Logic also told him that his and Celia's situation was about as far from the situation into which he'd been born as it was possible to get, but that didn't seem to matter. He wanted to be the kind of father to his child that his father had been to him. He wanted to be the kind of father who lived to see his child grow up. He wanted to be a father full stop. As they emerged from the clinic where they'd just had an appointment with the doctor to whom Celia's GP had referred her the feeling he had that what they were doing was dreadfully wrong was even stronger.

The sight of all those children's drawings papering the walls of the waiting room—which seemed so insensitive it had to be deliberate, as if testing the strength of the decision made by the people who'd wait there—had practically torn his heart out.

When they'd gone into the appointment itself and the ultrasound had shown a heartbeat, all he'd been able to think through the fog in his head was that that tiny little fetus was his child. *His child.* A weird kind of force had slammed into him, something that was instinctive, primal and surely had a lot to do with evolution, making his entire body shake with the strength of it.

And when the doctor had explained the procedure she recommended, his stomach had curdled and his chest had felt as if it had a band around it, squeezing tighter and tighter until he felt as though he could barely breathe. By the time she was through he'd just wanted to drag Celia the hell out of there.

Not that Celia had seemed in any way as affected by the appointment. She'd sat there, a bit pale, yes, but calm and composed, asking questions in a cool voice that suggested she was still as sure as she'd ever been and wasn't suffering anywhere near the kind of mental turmoil he was.

But what could he do about it?

He'd told her he was fine with the decision she'd made. He'd convinced himself it was the right thing to do, and he still stood by that. With his head, at least, which knew that he had to be fair and not put her in an even more difficult position.

His heart, however, was wondering if he could let her go through with it without at least telling her how he felt. If he could live with himself if he didn't at least mention it.

With the battle still raging in his head, he held the door to the street open for Celia and then followed her out. He spied a pub across the road and thought that never had he seen a place more welcome.

'I don't know about you,' he said, shoving his hands through his hair as if that might wipe the past half an hour from his memory, 'but after that I could do with a drink. What do you say?'

When she didn't answer, he stopped. Turned. To see her standing on the pavement looking pale, drawn and miserable.

'Are you all right?' he asked, which had to be the dumbest question of the century because she obviously wasn't all right at all.

'Not really.' Her voice was rough. Cracked. Filled with despair.

'What's wrong?'

Her eyes welled up, her chin began to tremble and she clamped her hand to her mouth. 'Oh, *God,*' she mumbled, and it sounded as if the words were being wrenched from somewhere deep inside her.

'What is it?' he asked, his heart hammering with alarm and who knew what else.

'I'm so sorry, Marcus,' she said wretchedly, 'but I don't think I can go through with it.'

And then, just as he was identifying that something else as hope, relief and a crazy kind of elation, and just as he was thinking that however complicated things were going to be he'd do his damnedest to make sure they'd be all right, she burst into tears.

Celia barely noticed Marcus taking her arm and making for the garden that filled the middle of the square. She was too busy crying like the baby that up until she'd seen the ultrasound she'd been so convinced she didn't want and making a complete mess of the handkerchief he'd thrust in her hand with a muffled curse.

He sat her down on a bench, wrapped a warm, solid arm around her shoulders and pulled her into him, murmuring that everything would be all right, and that just made her burst into a fresh bout of weeping.

What was she doing? she wondered desperately as she collapsed against him and sobs racked her body. Why was she crying? She never cried. Not even when she'd graduated top of her year and her father hadn't bothered to turn up to the ceremony had she shed a tear.

Maybe it was the stress of everything that had happened lately. The exhaustion of working so hard. The terror that she was falling apart and the relief to learn she wasn't. The shock of finding out she was pregnant. Being utterly convinced she wanted to have an abortion and then being knocked sideways by the thundering sensation that she didn't. Or maybe it was just her hormones going mental.

Whatever it was she couldn't seem to stop it. Tears leaked from her eyes, drenching the front of his shirt, her throat was sore and her muscles ached, and while she completely lost it Marcus just sat there calmly holding her, supporting her, comforting her in a way she'd never have expected.

Why wasn't he running a mile? Surely tears weren't his thing. Why hadn't he bundled her in a taxi and sent her home? She must be mortifying him. She was certainly mortifying herself. She'd thought that the night of Lily's dinner party when he'd come over to her flat, clapped eyes on her and his jaw had dropped in absolute horror was about as low as she could get, but this sank even lower. Her eyes would be puffy, her nose red and her skin blotchy, but that was nothing compared to the fact that by breaking down like this she was being so pathetic, so weak, acting so out of character.

And while the thought of falling apart in front of any man was distressing enough, to do so in Marcus' arms was enough to crush her completely.

Yet he didn't seem at all fazed by either her dramatic declaration on the pavement outside the clinic or her subsequent watery collapse. He was coping magnificently.

Surprisingly magnificently actually.

Although maybe it wasn't all that surprising, because now she thought about it he'd taken everything that had happened over the past week or so totally in his stride. He'd dealt with it all far better than she'd have imagined. Far better than she had, she thought, realising with relief that *finally* she seemed to be running out of tears.

As the sobs subsided and the tears dried up, she sniffed. Hiccuped. Then drew in a ragged breath. 'Sorry,' she said, her mouth muffled by his chest.

'You have nothing to be sorry for.' His words rumbled beneath her ear, the vibrations making her shiver.

Fighting the odd urge to snuggle closer, she unclenched her fingers from his shirt and drew back, wincing when she saw the black mascara smudges all over him. 'I do. I've ruined your shirt.'

He removed his arm from her shoulders and gave her a faint smile. 'I have others.'

His gaze roamed over her face and she went warm beneath his scrutiny. Squirmed a bit because the man was used to being surrounded by women who were gorgeous and heaven only knew what she looked like. A wreck most probably. But she could hardly whip out her mirror to check and rectify the damage. Not when presumably there was an important conversation about to be had. Like—

'Did you mean what you said back there?' he asked quietly, and she suddenly felt as if she were sitting on thorns.

Yup, like that.

She pushed her hair back and swallowed in an effort to alleviate the ache in her throat that might have been left over from her crying jag or might be down to the doubts now hammering through her. 'About not wanting to go through with it?' she asked, mainly to give her a moment to compose herself.

'Yes.'

His eyes were dark, his face once again unreadable, but there was an air of tension about him that told her it mattered. Well, of course it did. She'd probably just turned his life upside down, very possibly on the basis of a mere wobble.

She swallowed, her heart thumping as she tried to unravel the mess in her head. 'Maybe,' she said, rubbing her temples. 'I don't know.'

She wasn't lying. She didn't know, because she couldn't work it out. What on earth had happened back there? She'd been so sure she had it all figured out. That the course of action she'd started on was the right one.

Logically she thought that still. But emotionally...well, emotionally, she was all over the place, and had been pretty much ever since they'd turned up at the clinic.

She'd sat in that doctor's office, listening to what she'd said as if hearing the words through a wall of soup, and weirdly and worryingly her resolve had begun to weaken. And then the doctor had done an ultrasound and it had drained away completely.

How could everything she'd spent so long analysing be thrown on its head by one tiny little pulse fluttering at a hundred and sixty beats a minute? It didn't make any sense.

'I mean, it was fine when I thought it was just a bundle of cells or something,' she said, aware that Marcus was waiting for her to explain. 'But seeing the heartbeat...' She tailed off because how could she ever even *begin* to describe the feelings that had pummelled through her, and, in any case, why would he even want her to try?

'I know,' he said gruffly.

'And before that, all those pictures...'

'I understand.'

'It set something off inside me. Something instinctive.' She shrugged as if it were nothing but a minor blip, forced a smile to her face and shoved aside her doubts. 'But don't worry, I'm sure it'll pass.'

It had to, didn't it? Because she couldn't change her mind. She'd told him that she thought abortion was for the best and he'd agreed. He'd been quite firm about that. How selfish of her would it be to back out now and land him with the kind of commitment that lasted a lifetime, the kind he clearly didn't want?

He frowned. 'You really think so?'

Her throat went tight but she nodded. 'Of course. I mean, what the hell was I thinking? I can't have a baby.'

'Why not?'

Huh?

She stared at him, faintly taken aback. Had he forgotten the conversation they'd had only three days ago? 'We talked about this, remember?'

'We talked about why not having a baby was a good idea. We didn't discuss option number one at all.'

'No, well, we didn't need to. We were in agreement.'

'I have a feeling we still are.'

She blinked, a bit baffled by that. 'What?'

He looked at her intently, his eyes glinting, his jaw set with a determination she'd never seen before. 'Tell me why you think you can't have it.'

'Because I love my job. I want the partnership. I deserve it. It's what I've been working towards.' Hadn't they been through this already?

'Plenty of other women have children and a demanding job, don't they?'

'Of course they do.'

'So why not you?'

'It's not that simple, Marcus,' she said, wondering how

he'd forgotten about all the other reasons they'd come up with for why having this baby would be a bad idea.

'Isn't it?'

Exasperation slid through her. What was he trying to do here? Did he *want* her to change her mind? That didn't make any sense at all. 'You know it isn't.'

'OK, well, let's look at it hypothetically.'

'Hypothetically?'

He nodded. 'We didn't discuss it before, but I think we should now.'

'Isn't it a bit late?'

He shook his head. 'Now's the perfect time,' he said. 'So, hypothetically, if you'd decided to go with option one, what would you have planned to do when the baby was born?'

Worryingly and interestingly enough, she didn't even have to think about it all that hard. 'I'd have gone back to work,' she said, her heart beating fast and her head swimming for a second at what that might mean. 'Possibly hired a nanny. Maybe roped in my dad. He's been banging on about grandchildren long enough, and he's about to retire so presumably he'd have been prepared to step up to the plate. And Mum would have helped too, I'm sure. Hypothetically speaking, of course,' she added hastily, because it was a scenario she could now envisage all too clearly but one that could never happen because Marcus didn't want it to.

He stretched his legs out in front of him and crossed them at the ankles, staring straight ahead. 'And where would I have figured in all this?'

'You wouldn't have figured at all. Unless you'd wanted to. Which you wouldn't have because you don't even want a baby.'

'Don't I?'

Her heart squeezed but she ignored it. 'No.'

'Assume I do. For the hypothesis.'

Why was he doing this? she wondered, feeling uncharacteristically flustered. Was he making sure she'd thought through everything before going ahead? Or was it something else?

'OK, fine,' she said, her brain too frazzled to be able to work it through, 'but I don't see it would make any difference, because how could you help?'

'I could look after the baby when you go back to work.'

She stared at him in surprise. 'You?'

'Why not? My time is my own at the moment so it would make perfect sense.'

'What about your projects?'

'I can work on them from home.'

'You'd do that?'

'Yes.'

She didn't quite know what to make of that. 'Have you ever changed a nappy?'

He arched an eyebrow. 'Have you?'

'Well, no,' she conceded. 'But what about when the baby's six weeks old or something and has been crying non-stop all night and you realise just what you've taken on? Would you still want to stick around then?' And if he didn't, what would that mean for her career?

'Of course. Once I start something I don't give up.'

Except when it came to relationships, she thought, but before she could say anything, he added, 'And there's no way I'd give up on my child.'

'But wouldn't you mind?'

'What about?'

'About what other people might think if you stayed at home looking after a baby while I went back to work, for a start.'

'I don't give a crap what other people think.'

Which was admirable, but now it struck her that somewhere along the line this conversation had become less theoretical and more real so she steeled herself and said, 'But what does any of this matter? It's all totally irrelevant. Hypothetical.'

'Right.' He drew his legs back, sat bolt upright and swivelled so he was facing her, his jaw tight and his eyes practically burning into hers. 'But what if it wasn't?'

Her heart skipped a beat and her breath caught. 'I don't understand.'

'What if I said I'd changed my mind too?'

'I haven't changed—' She stopped. Stared at him. 'What?'

'You heard.'

'*Have* you changed your mind?'

He nodded. 'I have.'

'You want this baby?'

'I do.'

She reeled. 'But how? Why? You said you weren't fatherhood material and never would be.'

'I know I did.'

'So what happened?'

'Nothing happened. I just wasn't being entirely honest when I agreed with you that we should go for option number three.'

'Why on earth not?'

'Guilt, mainly.'

She stared at him. 'Guilt?'

'It's my fault you're pregnant.'

Her heart stumbled for a second. 'That's very noble of you, Marcus,' she said with small smile, 'but it does take two to tango. And we were careful. No one's to blame. It's just one of those things life likes to throw at you to really screw up your plans.'

'No, it really is. I opened the condom packet with my teeth. I think I might have ripped it.'

It was a possibility, she supposed, but, 'You don't know that you did.'

'Do you have a better explanation?'

'It could have been anything.'

'Doesn't matter,' he said resolutely. 'My condom, my application, my fault.'

For a moment she didn't know what to say. 'That's mad,' she managed eventually. 'None of this is anyone's fault.'

He shrugged. 'I should have been more careful. It's no excuse, but I wasn't thinking all that straight at the time.'

'No. Well, who was?' said Celia, going warm at the memory.

'Anyway, because of the guilt I decided that I'd go along with whatever you decided.'

With some difficulty she dragged herself back from the memory of that afternoon. 'So you lied?' she asked, frowning.

'Not exactly,' he said with a shrug. 'I simply didn't allow myself to think about what I wanted in case you wanted something different.'

Nothing simple about that, she thought, as she waded through it all. 'So given that,' she said, only about eighty per cent certain she got what he meant because the realisation that had she not said anything he'd have let her go through with it despite wanting the opposite was too much to handle right now, 'how do I know that your change of heart now doesn't simply reflect mine?'

Not much point in denying that she had had a change of heart any more, was there? Not when just the thought of holding her child made her heart practically burst from her chest.

'Because I've been having doubts for days.'

'So you think we should have this baby.'

'Yes.'

'But we don't like each other,' she said, knowing she was grasping at straws but trying to buy some time to absorb the enormity of where the conversation was heading.

His eyes glittered. Darkened. 'Don't we?'

Celia shivered at the heat that flared in his eyes but ignored it because the situation was complicated enough without adding chemistry into the mix.

'We live miles apart.'

'So move in with me.'

She gaped at him. On what level would that be a good idea? 'No.'

'Then how about into the house next door to me?'

'What?'

'I own it. I rent it out, but I can give the tenants notice and you can move in. Rent-free.'

'No way.'

'All right. Pay the rent. I don't mind. But it would be convenient, don't you think?'

'You've given this some thought.'

'None at all,' he said with a wry smile. 'I'm doing this very much on the hoof. But we have resources. Lots of them. The obstacles aren't insurmountable.'

He was formidable, she thought with a shiver. Determined and assertive and just a little bit overwhelming. Which was odd because a couple of months ago these weren't words she'd have used to describe him, although presumably he wouldn't have created a business worth millions if he hadn't been.

The combination was also very attractive, and she wished she could go back to thinking him laid-back, shallow and debauched because somehow those characteristics seemed a whole lot safer than the ones she'd seen in recent days.

With not a small amount of formidable determination of her own she pushed aside the realisation that she found him way more attractive now than she ever had before and concentrated on the conversation.

'I have a place of my own,' she pointed out, telling herself that just because what he suggested made frighteningly good sense it didn't mean she was ready to abandon her highly valued independence just yet.

'You have a pristine flat up four flights of stairs and there isn't a lift. Think about it.'

She did, and at the vision of herself struggling up them with a pushchair could see his point, not that she was going to admit it because the speed with which things were going if she did she could well find herself moved in to his house next door by the end of the week. 'How did you get to be so practical?'

'I always have been. You just haven't noticed.'

Seemed she hadn't noticed quite a bit. 'You're not going to suggest we get married or anything, are you?' she said, with the arch of an eyebrow and the hint of a grin.

He froze, a look of horror flashing across his face. 'Do you want me to?'

'*God,* no,' said Celia with a shudder, although part of her wondered what he'd have done if she'd said yes. 'My parents only married because my mother was pregnant with Dan and look what happened there. And despite the mess they made of things, and the effect it could have had on us, Dan and I have turned out pretty much OK, I think.'

The tension eased from his body and he shot her a quick smile. 'You turned out more than OK.'

'Nevertheless,' she said, going warm and knowing that annoyingly it had little to do with the heat of the midday sun, 'if we have this child you do know it would tie us together for ever, don't you?'

'Only in one respect. We'd still be free to pursue our own interests.'

No need to ask what those interests would be, she thought a bit waspishly as those photos of scantily clad Sardinians flashed into her head and the heat inside her faded. 'It would seriously cramp your style.' Not to mention hers, because, even though she didn't have much of one at the moment, at some point in the future she'd like to meet someone who didn't think of marriage as a fate worse than death.

'That's my problem to worry about.' He shifted on the bench, and as she caught a trace of his scent she tried not to inhale deeply.

'With the issue my parents have family parties would be a nightmare.'

'But manageable.'

'Do you have an answer for everything?'

'Not everything.'

'But most things.'

He gave her the glimmer of a smile. 'Do you have any other arguments to put forward?'

'No,' she said a little dazedly as she thought about it. 'I appear to have run out.'

'And?'

She tilted her head and stared at him, noting the dark intensity of his eyes, the set of his jaw, and wondering about both. 'You really want this, don't you?'

'Yes.'

'Why?'

'For the same reasons you do.'

Hmm. She doubted that, but she was hardly going to probe further. If she did then she'd have to go into *her* reasons, which she suspected went a lot deeper than the effect of a wall of paintings and an ultrasound.

But whatever his reasons, and however surreal today had been, however they were going to figure it all out, she knew what she wanted beyond the shadow of a doubt. And so, with her heart hammering, she took a deep breath and said, 'Then I guess we're going to be parents.'

CHAPTER TEN

'YOU'RE PREGNANT?'

At the volume of her brother's voice and the sudden hush that fell over the tapas bar where she, her brother and her sister-in-law were having supper and a catch-up for the first time since the happy couple had been back in London Celia winced. 'Not sure they heard you in the kitchen, Dan,' she muttered. 'Would you mind keeping it down a bit?'

'Yes, I bloody well would,' he said hotly. 'We've been here for over an hour, and you didn't think to mention it?'

She put down her fork, arched an eyebrow and shot him a look. 'And interrupt the fascinating and lengthy tales of your adventures on honeymoon?'

'You did go on a bit, Dan,' murmured Zoe, picking up her glass of wine and taking a sip.

Celia grinned. 'To tell you the truth, I loved hearing about what you got up to,' she said. 'Especially the bit where you got chased by a herd of angry alpacas. That's definitely one to bring out at your diamond wedding anniversary. And anyway, I'm mentioning it now.'

Dan frowned. 'How pregnant are you?'

'Twelve weeks, give or take a day or two.' She'd had the scan yesterday and when she'd seen those tiny little hands and feet and then been told that everything was progressing as it should had felt a mixture of relief, excitement and terror.

Marcus had been there too, the first time she'd seen him since they'd reversed their decision about the abortion. He'd sat next to her, asking questions and squeezing her hand and for a split second she'd felt this deep, *deep* longing that they were together. For each other, not just the baby. Which didn't make any sense whatsoever because they hadn't seen each other for four weeks and for all she knew he'd bedded half of London in that time. And while she knew that it was undoubtedly down to hormones, all in all it had been a rather peculiar, faintly unsettling quarter of an hour.

'Congratulations,' said Zoe, beaming.

'Thank you.'

Dan shot his wife a look. 'Why don't you sound as surprised as I am by this?' he asked suspiciously. 'Did you know? Two months in and do we already have secrets?'

Zoe shook her head and patted him on the arm. 'Calm down, Dan. Of course I didn't know. But when a woman declines alcohol and avoids the prawns it doesn't take a genius to work it out.' Then she shot him a wicked smile. 'And you might as well get used to the secrets thing because I have loads. You might even like some of them.'

His gaze locked onto his wife's and something flickered in his eyes that Celia didn't even want to try and analyse. 'Right,' he murmured, softening for a second before snapping his gaze back to her and glaring.

'You can stop looking and sounding all outraged,' said Celia, refusing to rise. 'This is the twenty-first century, you know. Women do get pregnant by accident and out of wedlock.'

'I know,' said her brother, shoving his hands through his hair and frowning. 'I'm just a bit stunned, that's all. I'd never have thought you...' He tailed off. Looked a bit bemused. Then rubbed a hand over his face as acceptance settled in. 'Do Mum and Dad know?'

'Not yet. I'll tell them soon.'

'Who's the father?'

Celia didn't see the point of not telling them. If Marcus

was intending to be as hands-on as he claimed they'd find out soon enough anyway. 'Marcus.'

Dan nearly fell off his chair. '*My* Marcus?'

'If you want to put it like that.' Although to be honest she didn't think he was anyone's. Nor, in all likelihood, would he ever be, given his track record, his comments on the subject and the look of horror that had filled his face when she'd jokingly asked if he was going to suggest they got married.

'I thought you couldn't stand each other,' said Dan, while Zoe merely smiled knowingly and helped herself to the last of the prawns.

Celia lowered her gaze and studied her non-alcoholic cocktail. 'Yes, well, things change,' she said, ignoring the sudden and unexpected urge to ask her brother if Marcus' aversion to commitment was simply down to an enjoyment of variety, because why would she need to know that?

And actually, things had changed quite a bit, she thought, turning it over in her mind as she twiddled her straw. Primarily her opinion of him. How she could ever have thought him shallow and pointless and irresponsible she had no idea. He might go out with—and probably sleep with—a lot of women but he was none of those things, and she'd been stupid and arrogant in her presumption that she had the measure of him all these years.

There was clearly a lot to learn about the father of her child. A lot of assumptions she had to ditch. So maybe she could do a lot worse than spend the next six months trying to figure out who Marcus really was, because if she was being honest he was turning out to be more fascinating than she'd ever have imagined.

'Since when?' asked Dan, slicing through her thoughts and making her head snap up.

'Since your wedding,' she said, and to her irritation she felt a blush storm into her cheeks.

Zoe flashed Dan a smug grin. 'Told you,' she said.

'So much for not ending the drought,' Dan muttered.

Celia snapped her gaze to him. 'What?'

'Before you, Marcus hadn't slept with anyone for six months.'

Blush forgotten, her jaw dropped as yet another assumption exploded into bits. 'Six months?'

'Exactly. We talked about it at the wedding. He had an ex who turned into a bit of a stalker. I told him that as you were the only single woman there and you weren't exactly each other's flavour of the month I didn't think that'd be changing. Seems I was wrong.'

'You were,' she murmured, intrigued and a bit distracted by the stalkery ex.

'I take it you're keeping it?' said Zoe.

'I am,' said Celia, dragging her thoughts back on track and deciding that there was no need to go into detail about the roundabout way they'd made that particular decision. Dan had only just got over his shock at finding out she was pregnant.

'And how the hell's that going to work out?' he asked.

She took a sip of water and thought about all the very practical—if faintly overwhelming—suggestions Marcus had made sitting on that bench in the square outside the clinic. 'I'm not entirely sure at the moment. We've tossed around a few ideas, but I guess we have six or so months to figure it out.'

And to figure out other things. Such as the truth behind his wicked reputation. Such as why he wanted to keep the baby. Such as whether she and Marcus had anything in common other than chemistry.

Her brother frowned. 'Have you considered the fact that Marcus has about as much stickability as an old Post-it note?'

'I have,' she said with a brief nod. Mainly in the moments of doubt she had when she wondered what the hell they were doing, if maybe a couple of years down the line she wasn't going to be left literally holding the baby. But then she'd recall what he'd said about never giving up once he'd started something, the steadfast determination etched into every inch of his face and the burn of his eyes, and her doubts eased somewhat.

'And he might be my best friend,' said Dan darkly, 'but *Marcus* and *responsibility* aren't words I'd put in the same sentence.'

'Oh, I don't know,' said Celia, unexpectedly finding herself bristling a bit on his behalf. 'I think you'd be surprised.'

Dan looked at her, his eyebrows shooting up. 'Would I?'

'I think he actually has quite a strong sense of responsibility,' she said, a bit taken aback by the strength of her desire to set the record straight. 'I mean, look at the way he made sure all his staff were taken care of when he sold his business,' she said, remembering something she'd read in the press weeks ago. 'Look at the plans he has now. Business mentoring? And that apprenticeship scheme thing for kids who've slipped through the system? He said it was his way of giving something back, and if that isn't a sign of recognising one's responsibilities I don't know what is.'

And then look at the way he'd taken care of her when she hadn't been well. The way he was stepping up to the plate now. All in all, she thought he was a remarkably responsible individual, even if Dan and Zoe couldn't see it.

Realising her heart was beating rather too fast and that she was feeling a bit fired up, she took a couple of deep calming breaths and gradually became aware that Dan and Zoe were staring at her.

'What?' she said, swinging her gaze between them as her pulse slowed and her indignation faded.

'Interesting,' said Zoe, regarding her thoughtfully.

'It is interesting,' she said firmly. 'Very. And I'm sure he'll make a success of it all.'

'I don't mean his plans,' said Zoe. 'Although those do sound good. I was referring to your defence of him.'

'I'm not defending him,' said Celia. 'I'm simply being honest.'

Zoe picked up a menu and smiled knowingly. 'If that's what you want to call it,' she said in an annoyingly conciliatory fashion. 'Now, who's having pudding?'

Two hours later, lying in the bath, enveloped in orange-blossom-scented bubbles and surrounded by a dozen flickering bergamot-scented candles, Celia dropped her head back and closed her eyes and pondered that disconcertingly knowing smile of her sister-in-law's.

What Zoe thought she knew Celia had no idea. She *was* being honest when she'd said all that stuff about Marcus being more responsible than everyone gave him credit for. And yes, maybe a teensy bit defensive, but so what? It didn't mean anything. She was just setting the record straight, and anyway, she was sure that if he ever learned that she'd leapt to his defence like that he'd split his sides laughing at her.

Zoe was too smug by half, thinking that she had the measure of their relationship. She didn't have a clue, apart, possibly, from identifying the chemistry, which now didn't matter all that much when there were so many other far more important life-changing decisions to be made.

Marcus might have alluded to the fact that they were still attracted to each other when they'd been sitting on the bench in that park, and, heaven only knew, he was in her thoughts a lot, sometimes all laid-back and smiling that lethal, lazy smile, sometimes all dark and intense, either way refusing to budge and making her pulse throb and her body tingle, but that didn't mean they were going to act on it, did it?

She, for one, had absolutely no intention of doing so. She had her child to think of and a relationship to build with its father, and sex complicating that and messing with her head was the last thing she needed.

How hard could it be to keep the attraction in hand anyway? It wasn't as if she were completely at the mercy of her hormones or anything. She was far too mature and sensible for that. It was simply a question of willpower, and that she had in abundance. So she'd easily be able to handle her attraction to him. She probably wouldn't even see that much of him over the next few months, apart from the occasions she intended they got together to work on that relationship. They were both busy, after all, and he had 'interests'…

Actually, she thought, not particularly wanting to contemplate Marcus and his 'interests', bearing that in mind, maybe she'd better get in touch with him to suggest fixing up the first 'getting to know you' session, because who knew how long it might be before they found a date they were both free?

Figuring out how he was going to adapt his lifestyle to incorporate looking after a child wasn't giving Marcus nearly as much trouble as figuring out what he was going to do about Celia.

The former wasn't a problem at all. Ever since the afternoon of Dan and Zoe's wedding, despite the concerted effort he'd made to move on, the thought of sex with anyone other than her was so off-putting he hadn't even bothered trying.

At first he'd found his lack of interest in anyone else infuriating, not to mention frustrating. Then he'd made himself relax because what could he do about it? He could hardly force himself to take things further, could he? Anyway, it was bound to be nothing more than a hiccup.

But if it was, then he was still hiccuping. And weirdly, not minding all that much. To his surprise he wasn't missing the thrill of the chase, the dating or even the sex. He'd been getting more than enough kicks from the work he'd been

throwing himself into. The apprentice scheme he was setting up was an idea he'd been toying with for a year or two
now, and it was great to be able to finally get it started. And
while unprofitable—at least in financial terms—it meant
so much that it felt good to be getting stuck in. Very good.

With a puritanism the Victorians would have been proud
of he was working hard and sleeping alone, and he'd never
felt more virtuous.

His thoughts about Celia, however, weren't virtuous at
all. They were wicked and filthy and sometimes came to
him at the most inappropriate of times. Such as during the
scan she'd had a couple of days ago. She'd hopped onto the
bed, and, with a wriggle that was sexier than it ought to be,
had lifted her top. It had been the least erotic of occasions,
yet at the expanse of taut, tanned stomach she'd revealed
he'd found himself tuning out the voice of the obstetrician
and wondering whether anyone would mind if he leaned
over and ran his hands and mouth across her skin.

She was in his head all the time. And not just with the
smiles she occasionally shot him. He found her fascinating. The contradictions that characterised her were intriguing. She was an intoxicating combination of strength and
vulnerability, pride and self-deprecation, confidence and
bewilderment.

Not that anyone got to see the softer side of her. He was
willing to bet everything he had that he was the only person who knew about her craving for her father's approval,
the only person ever to see her in the state she'd been in the
night they'd dashed to A and E. The only person to hold her
as she cried her heart out.

But even though he was now sufficiently not in denial
to know that he still wanted her—and quite desperately—
that didn't mean he was going to do anything about it. He
couldn't, could he? His relationships, however long they

lasted, always ended, and he'd never seen the point in keeping in touch.

If he and Celia had sex again, whether once, twice or a hundred times, when that side to their relationship burned out—as it inevitably would when he felt he needed to move on—it would make things unbearably awkward between them. Decisions they'd have to make would be clouded by things that were totally unrelated.

So they'd both be far better off ignoring the chemistry and concentrating on what was important here, namely the child.

Thank God she'd turned down his offer of his house next door. Heaven only knew what he'd been thinking when he'd suggested that. He might have been just throwing things out there but if she'd actually taken him up on the offer she'd have been living a mere stone's throw away instead of five miles, and his resolve to disregard the attraction that arced between them would have sorely been put to the test. Simply being in her vicinity did that as it was. A half-hour hospital appointment had been bad enough. Twenty-four-seven might just about do him in.

At least there was no reason to see her for a while, he thought, abandoning the Sunday papers for a moment, and reaching for his phone, which had just begun to ring. He'd use the time to shore up his defences and build up an immunity to her, so that when he next came across her he'd be rock solid, utterly immutable and ruthlessly focused.

Unlike now.

Feeling as dizzy and winded as if someone had thumped him in the jaw and then followed up with a punch to the gut, Marcus scowled and glared at the name on the screen.

For a split second he was tempted to ignore the call, let it go to voicemail and get back to her once those barriers were in place and he was immune. But that smacked of weakness and he had *some* pride, so he braced himself and hit the button. How disturbing could a phone call be anyway?

'Celia,' he said, pleased and relieved to note that he sounded cool and casual and not at all bothered by the fact that she'd rung.

'Hi,' she said, and, even though he could just about ignore the wave of heat that swept through him at the sound of her voice, there wasn't anything he could do about the goosebumps breaking out all over his skin.

He set his jaw, shifted his chair so he was sitting in a shaft of lovely warm sunlight and told himself that the sooner he made a start on building those defences, the better. 'How are you?'

'Fine, fine. You?'

Exhibiting worrying displays of a complete loss of control, but nothing he couldn't handle. 'Couldn't be better.'

'I'm so glad.'

She sounded glad. She sounded all warm and soft and seductive and he wondered what she was doing at half past ten o'clock on a Sunday morning. Where she was. What she was wearing… 'So what can I do to—I mean, for, you?' he said, his voice just as warm and soft and seductive, which *so* wasn't the plan.

'I'm ringing to see if you'd like to come over for supper some time.'

Mentally giving himself a slap and pulling himself together, he echoed, 'Supper?'

'That's right.'

'Why?'

'Well, I've been thinking,' she said, and he thought that it was a good thing that at least one of them was. 'You're the father of my child and it occurred to me that if we're going to do this together, it would make sense to discuss values. Opinions we might have about parenthood. And other stuff.'

What other stuff? Sex other stuff? His head swam for a

second and his pulse spiked and then he calmed down because, no, not sex other stuff, clearly. He was the only one
having trouble with that at the moment. 'I see.'

'I also thought that it would be a good idea to get to know
each other a bit better and learn to communicate without
the sarcasm. Food seemed like a good idea. So what do
you think?'

Marcus thought that was a fine idea. Maybe in a few
months' time, say around January, when he'd have had the
chance to build up those defences.

'Makes sense,' he said, carefully vague.

'Great,' she said brightly. 'So what about tonight?'

Marcus nearly dropped the phone. 'Tonight?'

'If you're available.'

He was. He was available a lot of nights these days. Not
that that was the point. 'What's the hurry?' he said, trying to maintain the cool and calm tone he'd been foolishly
quick to congratulate himself on only a couple of minutes
ago. 'We have months.'

'I know. But it's going to fly by and I'm busy every night
for the next week or so. So, are you free?'

Breaking out in a sweat, he shifted his chair out of the
sunlight. 'No,' he said abruptly. 'And I won't be for a while.'

There was a moment's silence and he inwardly cursed because he could have turned her down a little more tactfully.

'Oh,' she said flatly. 'Right. Well. When you do have a
moment free in your busy schedule let me know.'

Despite the flatness of her tone, he could hear the disappointment in her words, and as guilt swept through him his
conscience suddenly started prodding at him. All she was
suggesting was supper. Surely he could manage that. He always had before. Where was this idea that Celia somehow
posed a threat to him coming from anyway? It was ridiculous. *He* was ridiculous.

'Wait,' he said, hearing a rustling sound and guessing she was about to hang up.

The rustling stopped. 'What?'

He sighed and shoved a hand through his hair. 'Look, let me see what I can do.'

'Really?'

He closed his eyes, pinched the bridge of his nose and reminded himself that it was only supper. 'Really,' he said. 'What I had planned shouldn't be too difficult to get out of.' Which was true seeing as the only thing he had in his schedule was a night in front of the TV with his laptop.

'Won't she mind?'

At the hint of waspishness in her voice, Marcus found himself opening his eyes and smiling faintly. 'She won't mind at all.'

'One of these days you're going to come up against some-one who does.'

As the memory of his ex flashed into his head he shud-dered, his smile vanishing. 'Not in my plans.' He sat back and idly flicked through one of the colour supplements. 'And anyway, what was that you were saying about learn-ing to communicate without the sarcasm?'

There was another pause. 'Fair enough,' she muttered eventually. 'Sorry. Old habit.'

'If it's too tricky to resist, I'm more than happy to join in. I might even find myself having to make some kind of comment about the fact that you're willing to sacrifice a night's work for supper with me.'

She huffed, all contrition gone. 'You've made your point, Marcus.'

'Have I?'

'For the moment.'

'Until the next time you forget.'

'Until then,' she conceded after a moment.

'So, shall we say seven?' he said, thinking that that gave him enough time to throw up at least a few barriers.

'Sounds perfect,' she said.

'Although maybe it would be better if you came over here.'

'Why?'

'You don't cook and I've seen the state of your fridge.'

She hummed. 'Another point well made.'

'See you later, Celia.'

'I'm looking forward to it.'

As they hung up and the prospect of having Celia in his house, a mere floor away from his bed, sank in Marcus thought that she might be looking forward to tonight, but he wasn't. At all.

CHAPTER ELEVEN

'SOMETHING SMELLS GOOD,' said Celia, inhaling deeply as she stepped into Marcus' house just past seven and thinking that she wasn't just talking about the delicious aroma wafting from the kitchen.

Not that how heavenly he smelled or how gorgeous he looked was of any interest, of course. No. Tonight was purely about finding out what made him tick. Revealing a bit about how she ticked. Laying the foundations for a solid, long-term, *platonic* relationship. If she focused on that, she should be all right and wouldn't make any more mistakes about which things smelled or looked good.

'Roast beef,' he said, standing back as she brushed past him, his breath hissing softly through his teeth.

'With everything else?' she asked, wondering about that hiss and what it meant. If it meant what she thought it meant then he was finding the attraction that still sizzled between them as disruptive as she was. And if that *was* the case, then she could only hope that he'd come to the same conclusion as she had and had decided to ignore it, because if he had other ideas, such as wanting to explore it, then who knew what might happen? Her willpower was strong, but would it be strong enough to resist him if he suddenly grabbed her right now and kissed her?

'Naturally.'

She glanced at his mouth and her own watered. At the sound of supper, obviously, not at the thought of kissing him. 'Great,' she said with a bit of a strained smile.

'Go through to the kitchen. You know the way.'

Technically she did, so she walked down the hall and made for the kitchen. Metaphorically, however, she was floundering, not really knowing quite in which direction to head.

What on earth was wrong with her? She never normally had this much trouble with her self-control. She'd read about the brain sometimes going AWOL during pregnancy but it hadn't occurred that it would ever happen to her. The possibility that it had was unsettling. And it meant she had to be extra specially careful when she was around him.

He indicated that she should sit down, so she did. She ran her gaze over the table, laid for two—no candles, thank goodness—and then she turned it to the chef, who was busying himself with supper.

After switching the oven off, Marcus opened it, took the meat out and stuck a cloche over it, and then deftly dealt with a saucepan that was bubbling over.

His back view really was magnificent, she thought idly, her mouth watering at the aroma as she put her handbag on the chair next to hers and slowly let her gaze drift over him. In a purely objective fashion, of course, because objective appreciation of her host was allowed. It was good manners, in fact. Practically an obligation.

Whatever it was, she ogled the broad shoulders that tapered down to a slim waist that she envied now that her own was thickening, great bottom and long muscled legs, and let out a soft sigh of admiration.

Why was getting it on with him a bad idea again...?

'Drink?' he asked, turning around and making her jump. She went bright red, as if she'd been caught doing—and thinking—something she shouldn't have been. Which she had.

Wishing she could down a double gin and tonic for the sake of her nerves, Celia asked him for a tonic and to hold the gin, and once she'd quenched her suddenly rampant thirst decided it might be wise to do a little less of the ogling and a little more of the small talk.

'When did you become such a good cook?' she asked, putting her glass down and watching him lift a lid and peer into a cloud of steam.

'When I realised it was either that or starve. Then I discovered I liked it. I find it relaxing.'

'The ability to feed is a much sought-after quality in a man, I'd have thought.' In any man she ever ended up with, that was for certain, if he didn't want to go hungry.

'Not sure it's my most sought-after quality,' he said, shooting her a lethal grin over his shoulder.

Celia went warm, and half-heartedly tried to convince herself that it was merely down to the heat the oven was throwing out. 'No, well, I imagine not.'

He turned, leaned against the counter and shot her a quizzical look. 'Do you really not cook at all?'

'Toast and eggs I can do. Beyond that, not a lot. I usually grab something from the canteen at work and eat at my desk.'

'Even now?'

His gaze slid down her body, stopping at her abdomen, and she blushed. The oven again, undoubtedly. 'Even now.'

'It's really not that hard.'

She thought of her spotless kitchen and the devastation she would likely bring with a set of beaters or a food processor, and shuddered. 'I'll take your word for it.

'You should try it.'

Celia muttered sceptically beneath her breath and decided to move from her non-existent skills to his very much in-existence ones. 'Do you cook for your dates?'

'Sometimes.'

'I guess you'll have to pull out all the stops for the one you blew out this evening.'

He grinned and she ignored the jealousy stabbing at her chest. 'Four courses at the very least.'

'Hmm.'

'If there really had been a date.'

Her heart skipped a beat and just like that the jealousy vanished. Which would have worried her had she had the time or the inclination to analyse it, which she didn't. She was too giddy with relief. Disproportionately giddy, actually, which was something else that probably needed analysis. 'There wasn't?'

'Nope.'

She stared at him as she computed this. 'So why let me think there was?'

His grin deepened and a wicked glint appeared in his eyes. 'I couldn't resist. You're so determined to think the worst of me.'

She frowned and slowly rotated her tumbler between fingers. 'I don't think the worst of you at all.'

His eyebrows rose. 'No?'

She shook her head. 'No.'

'Wow, when did *that* happen?'

'I think it's been happening gradually. And then, of course, I heard about the drought.'

Now it was Marcus' turn to frown. 'The what?' he said, his smile fading.

'Your six-month period of abstinence.'

'How the hell did you hear about that?'

'Dan.'

His mouth twisted. 'Of course.'

'No wonder you were so desperate when I basically ordered you to ravish me amongst the runner beans.'

His dark eyes glittered and she shivered at the desire suddenly flaring in their depths. 'That had nothing to do with the drought and everything to do with you.'

She swallowed and sought a way to stop her body responding. 'I imagine you've been making up for lost time.'

'Why would you imagine that?'

'I've seen the photos.'

'Photos of what?'

'You and countless women.'

'Where?'

'In the press.'

'Right.'

He fell silent and she bristled with indignation. 'Is that all you have to say?'

'In these photos were me and these women naked and horizontal?'

'No, of course not.'

'Well, then.'

Well, then, what? Maybe she'd got the wrong end of the stick from the photos but that didn't mean Marcus hadn't been shagging his way round London like a thirsty man looking for a drink. After all, he hadn't been naked and horizontal with her, had he? Yet they'd still managed to have a pretty great time.

'I hope you're not going to say that I'm the only person you've had sex with in the last nine months,' she said, aiming for withering incredulity but, what with the unfathomable feeling of hope bubbling through her, failing dismally.

'That's exactly what I'm saying.'

'Really?'

'I've hardly been out recently, let alone swinging from the chandeliers.'

She sat back and stared at him. 'So why *did* you tell me you were busy tonight?'

His eyes were on hers. Steady, dark and intense. 'Because you *are* the only person I've had sex with in the last nine months,' he said, 'and I'm finding wanting a repeat of it increasingly on my mind.'

'Oh,' she said faintly.

'Quite.'

'That's the last thing either of us needs.'

'I know. Doesn't mean I don't still think it.'

As did she. All the time, if she was being brutally honest. But they'd just have to live with that. They weren't animals. They were rational, sensible people who knew what was good for them, and what wasn't. Still… 'Maybe we should keep off the subject of sex tonight.' It wasn't as if they didn't have plenty of other things to talk about. It should be a doddle.

'Good idea.'

Her stomach growled and his mouth hitched up into a small smile. 'And eat.'

'Even better.'

Keeping off the subject of sex was fine. Keeping from thinking about it was an entirely different matter. Ever since Celia had walked through the door Marcus had been aware of every move she made, no matter how tiny. All his senses felt heightened and it seemed to him that his body was trying to tune itself into hers or something. Whatever was going on it was odd. Frustrating. Deeply disturbing.

It didn't help that she kept groaning in ecstasy at the food he'd cooked. Every time she did, all he could think of was his bed upstairs and her on it. That was, when he wasn't mentally sweeping aside everything on the table and feasting on her down here instead.

As his body tightened uncomfortably Marcus thought that whatever Celia hoped to achieve by tonight, they wouldn't be doing it again, because this wasn't just 'supper', this was torture.

'This is delicious,' she said with a wide, warm smile that only strengthened his resolve to keep his distance once the nightmare of this evening was over.

'Thank you. Like I said, it's not hard.'

She put her fork down and took a sip of tonic water. 'So what have you been up to since I saw you last?'

'Work.' Driving himself insane.

'Is that all?' She arched an eyebrow and grinned. 'Careful, Marcus, you might turn into me.'

'To compensate I also spent a couple of days climbing in the Peak District.' In the hope that the physical exertion might result in mental exhaustion, and he'd be able to go five minutes without thinking about her. Not that it had worked.

Her eyes widened. 'I heard Dan took it up a while ago, but I didn't know you climbed too.'

'There's a lot you don't know about me.'

'And that's what tonight's all about.'

It was, and he could do a lot worse than focusing on that rather than the way her hair shone and her eyes sparkled. Because conversation was easy enough, wasn't it? And with any luck it would make the time fly. 'What about you?'

She shrugged and gave him a self-deprecating grin. 'Work, mainly.'

He returned the grin. 'Goes without saying.'

'But I also had supper with Dan and Zoe last night.'

'How was their trip?'

'It sounded fantastic.'

'Did you tell them about the pregnancy?'

She nodded. 'I did.'

'How did Dan take it?'

'Oh, fine,' she said nonchalantly. 'Eventually.'

Marcus went still, the hand holding his fork freezing midway to his mouth. 'Eventually?'

'For a moment I think he wanted to punch your lights out, but, realising it's not really any of his business, he got over it quickly enough.'

He frowned and put down the fork. Hmm. He should have guessed that while Dan would be fine with him dating Celia, he might not be so fine about the fact that his best mate had knocked up his sister.

But as that was a conversation he wasn't particularly looking forward to and didn't need to worry about tonight he put it from his mind. 'Do your parents know yet?'

'I rang them today.'

'And what did they say?' he asked, and braced himself for the news that her father, like son, had taken it badly and was bearing down on him even as they sat there.

'My mother was beside herself with excitement, and offered her full support and help.'

'And your father?'

Celia's smile turned wry. 'Ah, yes, well, after declaring himself delighted you'd taken him up on his suggestion, he said something about one out of three being a start. Not exactly being a new man, though, he wasn't quite so forthcoming with an offer of support and help. But he seemed pleased enough.'

'One out of three?'

'The baby. Marriage and a proper home being the other two.'

'Do they mind about you not being married?' he asked, thinking it best to avoid the subject of homes if he didn't want to have to discuss and retract the offer he'd made her in a moment of giddy recklessness.

'Surprisingly not,' she said, and then paused as if a thought had crossed her mind. 'Although I imagine that neither of them have much faith in the institution after what they went through so maybe it's not all that surprising.'

'They've never remarried, have they?'

Celia shook her head. 'No. I think my mother's too scarred by the experience and my father's having too much fun leching after twenty-five-year-olds.'

'Did the divorce scar you?'

She started as if startled by the question. 'Me? Oh. Well.

Not really. I mean, I was fourteen when they finally split and it was pretty horrendous but things had been awful for years. Dad had been having affairs practically since the ink was dry on the marriage certificate although I don't think Mum found out until a few years later. But I've nothing against marriage as a concept, and I'd quite like to do it one day. Although with things the way they are,' she said, indicating her abdomen with a wave of her hand, 'I can't see myself doing anything about that for a while.'

'No,' he muttered, a stab of guilt prodding him in the stomach as he collected up the plates and cleared the table.

'So what's put you off marriage?'

Marcus picked up a dish in the middle of which sat a chocolate tart, then sat down and used the business of cutting it into slices and sliding one onto the side plate she was holding up to think about just how open he wanted to be. The answer to which was, not a lot. 'What makes you think I'm against marriage?' he hedged.

She put her plate down and grinned. 'The look of horror that you had when I brought it up.'

'Right.'

'So?'

He shrugged and decided there wasn't any harm in telling her. It wasn't as if he had a problem with it or anything. It was just the way things were. 'I'm not against marriage in general,' he said, serving himself a slice. 'Just for me.'

'Why?'

'I've seen the damage that love can do. I am the damage. Or at least, I was.'

She nodded thoughtfully, presumably remembering the shocking stories about him that he knew Dan had regaled her with. 'So you steer clear of love too?' she said, taking a mouthful of tart and groaning softly in appreciation.

'Yes,' he muttered, giving his head a quick shake to dispel the faint feeling of dizziness. 'Although it's never been an issue because I've never been in love. But if I ever am I'll resist it with every bone in my body because in my experience love is messy and tragic and who needs that kind of hassle?'

'And that's where we differ,' she said, smiling wistfully and scooping up another bit of tart. 'Because I've never been in love either but from what I've seen it's lovely and so I'd like to experience it some day.'

Suddenly losing his appetite for pudding, Marcus sat back and ignored whatever it was that shot through him at the thought of her with someone else, because that she would be eventually was inevitable. 'I'm sorry,' he said gruffly.

'For what?'

'Putting you in this position.'

'Oh, it's fine,' she said airily. 'Now I'm beginning to come to terms with the reality of a baby I've mentally rearranged a few things.'

'Love and marriage being amongst them.'

'I'm not sure there's a lot you can do about love, but marriage was only a very vague goal anyway.' She grinned. 'So you don't need to worry—I won't be hassling you on that front. Unlike some, I imagine.'

Marcus frowned. 'What are you talking about?'

'I heard you have a stalker ex.'

Oh. 'Dan again?'

'Yup. And I have to say I'm completely agog. So come on, spill.'

'You want details?'

She arched an eyebrow. 'Of course I do. Think of it as part of the "getting to know you" thing.'

'OK,' he said, figuring he had no real reason not to tell her. 'I met her at a party and we went out for two months.'

'A whole two months?' she said dryly. 'A record, surely.'

Marcus shot her a look.

'Sorry,' she added, not sounding sorry at all.

'She wanted more. I didn't. We stopped seeing each other.'

'You dumped her?'

He shifted on his chair but he couldn't get comfortable. The memory of Noelle the Nutcase giving him hives probably. 'Yes.'

'And then?'

'She wouldn't accept it.'

'So what did she do?'

'Kept calling, texting, emailing. She turned up here once or twice, and at the office a bit more.'

Celia grimaced. 'How mortifying.'

'It wasn't the most pleasant of experiences,' he said, which had to be the understatement of the century. 'When she broke in here, arranged herself on the bed and waited for me to get home, I had to take it to the police.'

'And then what happened?'

'She was issued with an order to stay away both physically and electronically.'

'Has she stuck to it?'

'Thankfully.'

She hmmed. 'I can see why you'd be wary of getting involved after something like that.'

'Quite.'

She regarded him thoughtfully for a while and then leaned forwards. 'So tell me, Marcus, given your abhorrence of commitment, why do you want this baby so much?'

Where that had suddenly sprung from he didn't know, but the question didn't come as a huge surprise. 'It's hard to explain.'

She winced. 'I know the feeling.'

'Not just the ultrasound and those pictures for you, then?'

She shook her head. 'No. Although that afternoon was the key that unlocked everything, if that makes sense.'

'More than you probably realise.'

She put down her spoon and fork together on her spotlessly clean plate and bit her lip. 'For me I think it was a combination of things, really. My friends marrying and starting families. And then that thing my dad said about my age. It got into my head sort of insidiously and then stayed there, niggling away. I mean, I know I still have time, but after we made the decision to go for the abortion, I kept thinking what if this is my only chance? What if I got rid of this baby and I never got pregnant again? Would I regret it? And if I did, would I be able to live with the regret?' She shrugged and smiled, although there wasn't any humour in it. 'Silly, huh?'

'Not at all.'

'So what was it for you? Don't tell me you were envious of your friends settling down and having kids.'

'No.'

'And age wouldn't be an issue, so what was it?'

'Some stuff going back a while.'

'What kind of stuff?'

While he'd been absolutely fine with talking about love and marriage, this was veering into territory that would make him sound like a sentimental sap. 'Just stuff,' he muttered, hoping she'd leave it but knowing she wouldn't.

Celia tilted her head and looked at him. 'Come on, Marcus, I told you my reasons. You can tell me yours. Come to think of it,' she added contemplatively, 'you already know a lot more about me than I do about you, and didn't you once say you were all for equality?'

He had, and, after what she'd just told him, maybe he owed her the truth in return. Besides, if he carried on protesting she'd read more into his reluctance than there was to be read.

'Fair enough,' he said, sighing and running a hand along his jaw as he wondered where to start. 'Becoming a father

THE BEST MAN FOR THE JOB

isn't something I'd ever have chosen to do,' he said finally. 'But presented with the possibility, it opened a box for me too. Mainly to do with my father and our relationship.'

'Which was good, right?'

'Very good. I kept thinking about my childhood—which I remember as being improbably idyllic—and was filled with the overwhelming need to recreate it. I guess I'd like to have that father-child bond again, albeit from a different angle.'

'What if it's a girl?'

'Doesn't matter.'

'And the sacrifices you'll have to make?'

'Those don't seem to matter either. My lifestyle's already changed for one reason or another and I find I don't mind at all. You know, maybe I've been waiting for something like this to happen.'

Her eyebrows shot up. 'An accidental pregnancy?'

'Not exactly, but something that makes me evaluate my life.' Which was something he'd been doing quite a bit of actually. Recently the thing Dan had said about Marcus turning into Jim Forrester had been gnawing away at him. Did he really want to be fifty and chasing every woman he could? No, he didn't, so maybe once things had settled down he'd look at embarking on a proper relationship. One that might cure him of his inconvenient and impossible attraction to Celia.

'Do you miss him?'

Marcus shrugged and twirled the stem of his wine glass, watching the dark red wine swirl around. 'It's not too bad any more.'

'But you did for a while?'

'Like a missing limb.'

'And that's why you went off the rails.'

He nodded. 'Mainly.'

'And what about your mother? Do you miss her?'

Something inside him chilled a little and he abandoned his glass to pick up the knife and point it at the tart. 'More pudding?'

Celia shook her head. 'No, thanks. It was delicious, though.'

'Coffee?'

'No, thanks,' she said again, only this time with a tiny frown.

'Tea?'

'Nothing, thank you. Except an answer. That would be nice.'

It wouldn't be nice at all, he thought darkly, clearing the table and refusing her offer of help. Which, with hindsight, was probably a mistake because instead of being busy with dishes, she had time to wonder.

'Why are you avoiding the question, Marcus?' she asked, and he could feel her eyes on him.

'Because it's a tricky one to answer,' he muttered.

'Why?'

With a deep sigh, Marcus abandoned the crockery and turned to lean against the counter. 'Following my father's death neither of us were very good at dealing with our grief,' he said, folding his arms across his chest as if that might somehow suppress the memories. 'I went wild. She withdrew into herself. Ultimately she'd loved him so much she couldn't live without him. Literally.'

She nodded, her eyes filling with sympathy, compassion and pity, and he couldn't work out whether it pissed him off or made him grateful. 'I heard. I'm sorry.'

He shrugged. 'Nothing to be sorry about. She just couldn't go on without him, that was all.'

'She must have been in a very bad way.'

'She was. She was deeply depressed, even though I don't think she realised it. I certainly didn't.'

'No, well, how could you have?'

The guilt struck him square in the chest and his jaw tightened. 'If I'd been less hell-bent on self-destruction I might have.'

'She'd have found a way whatever you'd done.'

'If I'd at least tried she might have thought I was worth sticking around for.'

For a moment there was absolute silence and Marcus wished he could take back the words because he'd said too much. Way too much.

'I'm sure that wasn't it,' she said softly.

'It was,' he said bluntly. 'She left a note. Basically saying that she loved me and that she realised she'd be leaving me behind but that it wasn't enough to stop her.'

Celia looked stricken and a dozen different emotions flickered across her face. 'Oh, God,' she murmured.

He arched an eyebrow. 'You did ask.'

'I know I did.'

'Regretting it?'

'Not for a second.'

He gave her a dry smile. 'Hardly the best of gene pools, is it?'

'Oh, I don't know,' she said, running her gaze over him and, whether she knew it or not, making him forget that horrible couple of years and return his focus to her.

He watched her eyes darken, heard her breath catch, and desire hit him like a blow to the chest. His hands itched. His mouth went dry and he was a second away from hauling her up from the chair and into his arms when she blinked, snapping the connection and making him recoil.

'So how did you get from hurtling off the rails to where you are now?' she said a little hoarsely, sounding as shaken as he was.

Marcus gathered his wits and thanked God Celia had had the sense to pull them back from the edge. 'Just after my mother died and I was spinning really out of control, a friend of my father's basically took me in hand. He put me to work in one of his companies, a brokerage. It turned out I had an affinity for stock picking and I moved up until I set up my own business. The rest you know.'

'Didn't any of your own friends try to help?'

'Dan did a bit. But we were eighteen, nineteen. I was determined to raise as much hell as I could and I was very good at it. There was nothing he could have done.'

'Is that why you're setting up this scheme to help people like you once were?'

'Yes.'

'Paying it forward.'

'In a small way.'

'And what about the business mentoring and the angel investing?'

'I had no idea you were listening so closely.'

'I was listening.'

'Right,' he said, wondering why the thought of her listening would make his heart beat this hard and this fast. 'Well, that's because I enjoy taking risks and making money.'

Celia gave him a smile that was hot and wicked and threatened to blow his noble intentions to keep his hands off her to smithereens. 'I'm glad to hear you're not all good.'

There was a crackling silence, and as they looked at each other, with heat and tension filling the space between them, all Marcus could think about was how much he wanted her. How much he always had. To hell with what was right or wrong. Screw the consequences. He wanted her, and she wanted him, and he, for one, was going to go mad if they didn't do something about it.

'Are you?' he said softly, taking a step towards her and seeing her eyes widen with alarm.

She stood up, nearly knocking her chair over in her haste, and grabbed her bag. 'Of course,' she said way too brightly, edging back and keeping the distance. 'Just think of your reputation.'

He was having trouble thinking about anything but her and what he wanted them to do together. 'I know it comes fifteen years too late,' he said, keeping his eyes on hers, 'but I'm sorry about making up the bet.'

'Fine,' she said quickly. 'And I'm sorry about what I said about using you.'

'Were you? Using me, I mean?'

'No.'

'So why did you say you were?'

'I was confused. Overwhelmed.'

'By what?'

'By you and the effect you have on me,' she said breathlessly.

His pulse spiked and a bolt of desire thumped him again. 'And what effect is that?'

'You know perfectly well.'

'It's entirely mutual, you know.'

She swallowed hard and took a breath, as if struggling for control. 'It's also utterly irrelevant.'

'Remind me why,' he murmured because for the life of him he couldn't remember.

'Sex would only make a complicated situation even more complicated.'

'Would it?'

'And the awkwardness when it fizzles out would be hideous.'

There was that, he thought with the one brain cell that was still functioning, but this tension, frustration, was pretty hideous too. 'Nevertheless, I have a suggestion.'

A tiny flicker of alarm leapt in her eyes. 'I don't want to hear it.'

'You don't know what it is yet.'

'It's something along the lines of getting it out of our systems so we can move on, isn't it?'

He gave her the glimmer of a smile. 'The idea has merit, don't you think?'

'It's insane.'

'We could try it and see. It worked before, didn't it?'

'I should go,' she said, shaking her head as if to clear it.

'Should you?'

She nodded hard. 'Definitely.'

'This isn't going to go away, Celia, even if you do.'

'No, but if we're sensible, it'll be manageable.'

Sensible? Manageable? 'How?'

'We ignore it.'

'Not sure that's an option.'

'No...' she agreed a little desperately. 'OK, then, how about from now on we stick to meeting up in public?'

CHAPTER TWELVE

OVER THE COURSE of the next few weeks that was what they did.

They met in restaurants, bars and various parks. Despite having known each other for nearly twenty years, so much of that time had been clouded with animosity that they'd never really talked.

Now, though, they did nothing but.

They discovered that, while they disagreed about many things, about the big things, the important things, they were more or less on the same wavelength. They also found they had plenty in common. An interest in obscure French cinema. A deep dislike of cats. A love of chilli and being terrible patients, amongst many other things.

And, of course, the still-scorching chemistry.

That hadn't gone away, thought Celia, blotting her lipstick and trying not to think about the evening she and Marcus had had fish and chips and he'd reached out to rub away a blob of ketchup at the corner of her mouth.

If anything it was getting worse, because mature and sensible and not at the mercy of her hormones? Who the hell had she been kidding? Her hormones were going so mental that she couldn't believe that at one point she'd seriously thought that ignoring what was going on between her and Marcus was an option.

It had taken all her strength to walk away that night she'd gone for supper at his house. She'd been so very tempted to simply fall into his arms and yield to the need that had been clawing away at her, especially when he'd so clearly been up for it. But some sixth sense had warned her against it, and thank *God* she'd got out of there before she'd given in to temptation.

Their conversation that night had been unsettling. Not the subject matter—although that had revealed more about him than she ever could have imagined—but the way she'd responded to it.

When he'd asked what her family thought about the pregnancy it had occurred to her that he didn't have anyone to tell, and her heart had wrenched. When he'd told her he had no intention of falling in love or ever marrying because of his experience, it had wrenched a little more. And when he'd been talking about his mother's suicide and the note she'd left, well, that had just about torn her apart because it clearly affected him, making him think that somehow he wasn't good enough when he was. He so was.

It had been disconcerting, because Marcus wasn't supposed to tug at her heartstrings. He wasn't supposed to have as much depth as he did, although quite why he wasn't when he'd been through such a tough time she didn't have a clue.

She wasn't supposed to like him so much either, but there was another anomaly, because she did. A lot. He made her laugh. Entertained her. Challenged her and made her think and question and argue. So much so that the days they were meeting up she woke up on a high and then spent the rest of the day fizzing with excitement and counting down the hours until she could leave to go and see him. Sometimes she even left work early, which, given that she was meant to be doing everything she could to win the partnership, was madness.

She ought to be wary of seeing him, not excited. Because every time they met up the occasions were underscored with such a strong current of tension that she'd started to think that perhaps they *should* have gone to bed that night. Perhaps Marcus had been right and it *would* have got things out of their system. Maybe the fact that they hadn't was what was making the idea of it so compelling.

Frankly, it was hard to see how sex would have made things any worse because the tension between them was sky-high. Every date that wasn't a date was filled with fleeting touches. Laden looks. Conversation that tailed off. Sizzling, thundering silences and a hundred electrically charged moments before they said an awkward goodbye and each headed home separately.

Not that it ended there, for her at least. Marcus was in her head pretty much constantly. Her dreams were full of him, and during the day she frequently found herself storing tiny things away to tell him later.

She didn't know how he was dealing with it all, but for all her fine words about sense and manageability her resistance was rapidly weakening. She couldn't remember why sex with him had seemed like such a bad idea. She'd been thinking it might be a very good idea indeed for a while now. Now she was thinking that tonight, finally, she'd like to do something about it.

It might be reckless and it might be rash, but she'd had enough of the excoriating frustration and the agonising tension. She'd had enough of the sleepless nights and the feverish dreams that assailed her when she did eventually manage to drop off. It wasn't doing her nervous system any good at all and, heaven knew, she didn't want her palpitations to reappear.

So today she had a plan. This afternoon she'd find out whether she'd got the partnership, then later she and Marcus were going out for dinner at a three-Michelin-starred restaurant. And whether they were celebrating or commiserating, one thing was for certain: they were going to end the night together, in bed and having fabulous, hot, sweaty sex.

* * *

Tonight Marcus was going to end this 'getting to know you' crap.

He stood at the basin in his bathroom, leaned forwards and wiped away enough condensation from the mirror to be able to see his reflection, which was actually pretty grim. No surprise there, he thought darkly as he picked up a can and squirted a ball of foam into his hand. He'd been feeling grim for days. Tense and grumpy and frustrated as hell.

With hindsight, agreeing to her plan to get to know each other had been nuts. Going along with it had been even more insane. Where the hell had the intention to make that night she'd come for supper a one-off gone? When she'd suggested they stick to meeting up in public and he'd said fine without a moment's consideration, what on earth had he been thinking?

Shaking his head in disbelief and wondering when exactly he'd lost his mind, Marcus began lathering up his face.

As if simply meeting up in public was the way to handle the scorching attraction that sizzled between them. Hah. They might not be able to act on their feelings in public but that didn't make them go away, did it? No. It was simply making them worse. For him, at least.

He had no idea how Celia was dealing with it but he was handling it badly, because over the past three weeks or so that they'd been seeing each other he'd been finding it increasingly hard to resist her.

At first it had been fine. Well, not exactly fine, but he'd told himself that he could keep his impulses under control, and he'd more or less succeeded knowing it was a bad idea and, more importantly, why. Lately, though, they met up and it was all he could do not to grab her arm, hail a taxi and take her home. He was in a permanent state of confusion and arousal, and it was driving him crazy.

Picking up his razor, Marcus tilted his head and cut a

swathe through the white cream and winced as he nicked his jaw. Dammit, he *had* to put a stop to these meetings. They'd been an indulgence he could ill afford and it was time to end them.

Anyway, the whole idea behind them in the first place had been to get to know each other and by now they knew plenty. Too much, in fact. Celia had told him things he didn't want or need to know. Things that had him wondering how on earth he could ever have thought her an uptight, judge-mental pain in the arse. Things that had him thinking that, on the contrary, what with her sharp wit and her spot-on insight, her warmth and her self-deprecation, she might be rather wonderful.

In return he'd found himself telling her things he'd never told anyone. Big things. Small things. Either way, a lot of things. He'd given her so many little pieces of himself over the past three weeks, in fact, that she nearly had the whole.

As much as he might have wanted to prevent it she'd got under his skin. And he could tell himself all he liked that it was merely down to the fact that he hadn't had the chance to build up those all-important defences, but that didn't eradicate the feeling that even if his defences had been the height of Everest she'd simply have bulldozed them down.

He didn't know what it meant. Wasn't sure he wanted to know.

What he wanted, he thought, finishing up and wiping his face clean, what he *needed,* was space. A bit of distance and time to get some perspective and figure out what was going on here. And then, if necessary, put a stop to it.

So after tonight that would be that. He'd tell her he needed a break, and tomorrow he'd make plans to go away.

If he still lived by the principles he'd had at eighteen—and right now he wished he did—he'd have cancelled this evening. But he knew how important this partnership deal was for her and how hard she'd worked for it. And he knew that despite her apparent confidence that it was in the bag, that she'd worked so hard it had to be hers, she was nervous about the outcome.

So they'd go for dinner as planned and he'd order a bottle of champagne just in case she wanted half a glass whatever the result, he'd be as charming as she was expecting him to be, and after that, as he'd done so many times before, he'd bid her goodnight and put her in a taxi.

And then tomorrow, in a bid to get that distance, he'd be off.

Celia stood on the pavement outside the restaurant from which she and Marcus had just emerged, her body buzzing and her pulse racing. Not with delight about getting the partnership, which, if she was being honest, didn't come anywhere near the thrill of being out and celebrating it with him, but with the thought of what, hopefully, was coming next. Which was, with any luck, her.

Dinner had been sublime. The heavenly array of food, the seductive lighting and incredibly romantic atmosphere and above all, Marcus, who'd gone out of his way to make tonight special.

He'd ordered her a bottle of champagne and then asked for it not to be opened so she could keep it and drink it when she was back on the hard stuff. He'd told her to have whatever she wanted or everything, if that took her fancy. He'd asked her all about her meeting this afternoon, and had seemed more enthusiastic about the fact that she'd got the partnership than she was.

And now... Well, now, come hell or high water, she was going to take him home with her.

He wanted her; she knew he did. Even if they hadn't spent the past three weeks communicating it with everything other than words, every now and then this evening she'd looked up to find him watching her, his eyes blazing with hunger and desire before the shutters snapped down and he made some comment designed to make her laugh and forget about what she'd seen.

But she couldn't forget. Nor did she want to because she'd hungered for him for so long and she couldn't stand the frustration any longer. She didn't think he could either.

'Thank you for a lovely evening, Marcus,' she said, her voice husky with the desire that she couldn't be bothered to hide any more.

He glanced at her, his jaw tight and a faint scowl on his face as he shrugged on his jacket. 'No problem.'

'And thank you for supper.'

'Least I could do,' he said, adjusting the collar and then tugging at the cuffs of his shirt beneath his jacket.

And, OK, so his mood seemed to be worsening with every second they stood on the pavement, which wasn't particularly encouraging, but what the hell? He could always say no. She'd been thinking about this for what felt like for ever and she had to give it her best shot because she'd never forgive herself if she didn't.

'Marcus,' she said, her heart thundering and her mouth dry as she inched towards him.

'What?' he said, thrusting his hands in the pockets of his trousers and looking down at her unsmilingly in the darkness.

She stepped closer and fought the temptation to sway slightly as her body responded to the magnetism he exuded, and then took a deep breath. 'Will you come home with me?'

Marcus wanted nothing more than to go home with her. And nothing less.

Tonight had been agony. Celia had sparkled from the moment she'd sat down at the table where he'd been waiting for her, and he'd known practically right then and there that he was doomed. That it was going to take every drop of his control to put her in a taxi alone at the end of the night.

But he'd got through it. And had thought he'd succeeded.

But dammit, he should have known that Celia would suggest something like this. He'd seen the desire in her eyes all evening, not banked as his was, but alive and burning and so very tempting.

He should have realised that excitement and the high of success would spill over into recklessness. He should have been prepared. Even better he should have cancelled in the first place, he thought grimly, mentally cursing every principle he possessed.

But as he hadn't, right now he just had to be stronger, more resolute and more ruthless than he'd ever been before. For both their sakes.

'Stop it, Celia,' he said, his voice as rough as sandpaper with the effort of holding onto his control and not grabbing the next taxi that passed, bundling her in and clambering in after her.

'Why?'

'You know why.'

She tilted her head and her hair rippled, gleaming in the light of the street lamp, and he fought back the urge to reach out and wrap a chunk of it round his fingers. 'I thought I did,' she said softly, 'but now I'm not so sure.'

Then he'd make her sure. 'It would screw everything up.'

'Isn't everything pretty much screwed up anyway?'

His jaw tightened. 'And you want to make it worse?'

'I want to make it better.'

No. *He* was going to make it better. 'I'm going away.'

She stared at him, wide-eyed and momentarily speechless. 'Where to?'

'I don't know. Anywhere.'

Her eyes filled with understanding. 'I see. When?'

He'd have gone now if he had a plan, which he didn't

because right now he wanted her so badly he could barely *think*. Which was bad. Really bad. 'Tomorrow.'

'Then we still have tonight.'

'We'd be mad to even consider it.'

'You want it as much as I do.'

Of course he did. He was as hard as rock and had been since for ever, but even though his self-control was stretched more than it had ever been it was still holding firm. 'So what?'

'This has been brewing for weeks.'

'I know.'

'What's the point of resisting it any more?'

'There are a billion points.' Although he was damned if he could remember any of them.

'I'm tired of it, Marcus. And I know you are too.'

'I've never stayed on friendly terms with any of my exes,' he muttered, and then wondered what the hell that had to do with anything, because he wasn't seriously considering this, was he? God. No. He couldn't be...

'Nor have I,' she said. 'But one night does not an ex make.'

'What does it make?' he said, his head swimming as much with confusion as desire.

'I don't know. Heaven?'

Heaven sounded good. So good... 'And then?'

'Who knows?' she said with a small smile that just about undid him. 'But what if you were right?'

'About what?' he said, his voice sounding as if it came from a million miles away.

'Maybe we *should* try and get it out of our systems.'

'No,' he said, but the denial was weak. 'You're not think-ing straight.'

'Actually, I've never been thinking straighter. Avoid-ing it doesn't seem to be working, does it? So what other choice do we have but to confront it? Because it's not going to go away.'

'It has to.'

'What if it doesn't?'

If it didn't they'd have a lifetime of it, tearing them up inside.

At the thought of that Marcus went dizzy, his heart hammering and his stomach churning. A lifetime of this? How would he stand it?

Especially when he didn't even have to.

Collapsing under so much pressure, so much need, Marcus felt what was left of his self-control disintegrate. He'd clung on for as long as he could and he knew it was the worst idea in the world to take Celia up on her suggestion but he was only a man. He had his limits like everyone else and she was pushing him way past his.

He'd tried to resist, so hard, he had for months, but the pleading in her voice, the hunger in her eyes, the sense she was making when it was everything he wanted had chipped his resolve right away. He was a man at the end of his tether, and, really, she was right. What was one night?

'Whatever happens after,' she said, stepping closer, putting her hands on his chest and splaying her fingers, her proximity scrambling his head even more and making him feel quite weak, 'I know what I want, Marcus, and I know what I'm doing.'

'Do you?' he grated as the last of his resistance shattered and he gave in, body and soul. 'Really? Because I don't have a *clue* what I'm doing.'

And with that, he pulled her into his arms, one round her waist and the other at the back of her head, and crashed his mouth down on hers.

Her hands slid up his chest, burning a trail he could feel right down to his toes. She wound them round his neck and locked them there as she pressed against him.

She moaned and he pulled her tighter and it was as if someone had thrown a match on a tinderbox. Heat surged between them. Fire ran through his veins. His heart thundered and desire surged through his blood, thick and drugging and nearly making him forget where they were.

But not quite.

He pulled back, breathing harshly, and she whimpered.

'Don't stop,' she mumbled, pulling his head down and kissing him again.

'We have to,' he said, somehow finding the strength of will to unwind her arms from around his neck and peel himself away.

'No,' she protested. 'Why? Surely you're not going to turn all scrupulous on me *now*.'

'God, no,' he said, thinking he was too far beyond the point of return to come up with all the reasons they shouldn't be doing this.

'Then why?'

'Because for one thing,' he said, taking her arm and scouring the street, 'if we don't we'll be arrested for indecency, and for another we need to find a taxi.'

CHAPTER THIRTEEN

THE JOURNEY TO Celia's flat passed by in a bit of a blur, although not because they were going particularly fast.

In fact, after that first frantic kiss on the pavement during which she'd nearly gone up in flames with longing and relief because his strength of will was such a powerful force that for a moment she'd doubted her ability to break it, she and Marcus were now going achingly slowly.

The minute he'd slammed the door behind them and the driver had pulled away from the kerb, he'd slid an arm around her shoulders and pulled her to him. She'd leaned into him and lifted her hand to the back of his neck, and their mouths had met and they stayed like that, necking like teenagers as they crossed London, sharing long, slow, drugging kisses that blew her mind and obliterated her control.

At one point, she tried to straddle him, desperate for the feel and the friction of his hardness against the place where she needed it most. She didn't get very far, though. She'd just slid her leg over his and Marcus had just clamped his hand to her thigh to help her climb onto his lap, when a not so discreet cough from the taxi driver had them stopping in their tracks and sticking to kissing.

She was so dizzy with desire and desperation, so out of her mind with need, she barely noticed the taxi coming to a stop outside her building. When Marcus peeled away, her brain was too frazzled to be able to work out why until her head cleared enough to see that he'd got out and was thrust-

ing a couple of notes through the window and muttering
something about there being no need for change.

How she managed to get her key in the lock when her
hands were so shaky she didn't know. And as for climbing
all the stairs to her flat, well, since her limbs had turned
to water she must have floated. Either that or Marcus had
somehow carried her up as they carried on kissing.

But eventually, still entwined but now grappling at cloth-
ing, they made it through her front door, and she slapped at
the light switch before they stumbled into her sitting room
and tumbled down onto the sofa.

Marcus landed first. Celia followed, straddling him the
way she'd wanted to in the taxi. She shed her jacket and
her shirt while he shrugged off his and then his hands were
around her back unhooking her bra.

Shivering, although not with cold, she put her hands on
his chest, *finally* finding out what he felt like, and he in-
haled sharply, tensing beneath her touch. She splayed her
fingers, slid her hands over the sprinkling of coarse hair,
the hot skin over tight muscle and then the thundering of
his heart and she thought it couldn't be hammering nearly
as hard or as fast as hers.

Especially not when he moved his hands down round
her waist and up to cup her breasts. Heavier, thanks to the
pregnancy, and…oh, Lord, *super*sensitive. He brushed his
thumbs over her nipples and as sparks showered through
her she groaned and arched her back in an instinctive attempt to increase the pressure.

In response Marcus nudged her back and then bent his
head, and as he closed his mouth over her breast, his tongue
flicking back and forth, Celia yelped and nearly came right
then and there.

She'd never known anything like it, she thought dazedly,
staggered at the sensations coursing through her. She'd had
sex. Good sex. And not just with him. But this… This was

something else. She felt as if every nerve ending were tingling. As if every muscle were tightening and every cell were bracing itself for heaven.

Was it just her hormones or was it him?

Did she care?

Not really. All she cared about was doing this. Right now.

She thrust her fingers in his hair and brought his head up. Captured his mouth with hers and ground herself against him as he was grinding himself against her.

Enough. She couldn't take it any more.

And clearly neither could Marcus because he was lifting her onto her knees and shoving his jeans and shorts down. A second later he was running his hands up her stockinged thighs, brushing over the nubs of her suspender belt and groaning, and pushing her skirt up and ripping first one side of her knickers and then the other.

'You have something against knickers?' she mumbled against his mouth.

He choked out a laugh. 'Only yours.'

'They were expensive.'

'I'll buy you more.'

And then he slid a couple of fingers inside her and she couldn't remember what they'd been talking about. All she could do was bite her lip to stop herself from crying out, and try to cling onto some kind of control.

'God, you feel good,' he muttered.

'So do you,' she moaned. 'I need you, Marcus. Inside me. Now.'

It must have been the sob that accompanied the 'now' that told him of her desperation because within a second he'd slipped his fingers out of her, took himself in one hand and held her hip with the other, and whether she thrust down or he thrust up, she didn't know. All she knew was that just when she couldn't bear it any longer he was lodged deep

inside her, filling her and stretching her and she was losing
her mind with the pleasure spearing through her.

'Don't you think this was the best idea ever?' she panted
as he began to move and she with him.

'Not able to think,' he muttered, one hand clutching at
her hip and the other clamped to the back of her neck.

And then nor was she because he was slowly pulling out
of her and then driving into her over and over again, and
she could feel the tangle of feeling swelling inside her, her
head spinning faster and faster until she erupted, crying out
his name as she came and then again when, a second later,
he exploded deep inside her.

She collapsed against him, stars flashing behind her eye-
lids and her body weak and trembling, the rasp of his breathing the only thing she could hear.

'So,' she said dazedly once she'd got her breath back
and her heart rate had subsided. 'Would you say it's out of
your system now?'

Marcus laughed raggedly and shook his head before resting his forehead against hers. 'Celia, sweetheart, it's not
even looking for the exit.'

Giddy with relief she grinned and shifted and murmured
against his mouth, 'Then how about this time we *finally* get
naked and find a bed?'

Celia sat on her window seat in her bedroom, stared out
into the moonlit darkness as she listened to Marcus' deep
breathing from where he lay sprawled across her bed, and
thought that she might as well face it. She was head over
heels in love with the man.

She didn't know how or when it had happened, only that
at some point over the past two months or, more likely, fifteen years, it had, and that now she was aware of the fact it
was hard to imagine not being in love with him.

When she thought about the criteria she'd always considered important in a man, he fitted. In almost every way. He was strong, loyal and supportive. Hard-working, driven and ambitious. He had a strong sense of moral responsibility, played to his strengths and accepted his weaknesses. In short, he was amazing.

How had she not seen it before?

Smiling gently, still slightly stunned by the realisation she was nuts about him when only a short while ago she'd loathed him, Celia hugged her knees to her chest and grimaced when her tummy got in the way. So she stretched her legs out instead and crossed them at the ankles and thought about the way he made her feel. Apart from the sex, which was mind-blowing as well as eye-opening, he made her feel as if she could do anything, be anyone. He was the first person she wanted to turn to, whether with successes or failures. The first person she'd go to if she was ill, doubtful or needed a different take on something. The only person she wanted to love, live with and have a family with.

And the best, truly amazing, thing was, she was pretty sure Marcus was in love with her too. She'd felt it in his touch tonight when they'd made it to her bed. She'd seen it in his eyes. Heard it in his words. He'd explored her so thoroughly, so tenderly, lingering over the slight rise of her abdomen, almost as if he'd been worshipping her.

She was equally sure, however, that he wouldn't want to be in love with her, and that when he realised he was he'd reject it with everything he had. But that was fine. She wasn't planning on going anywhere for a while, even if he was. He was worth it so she'd wait. And not just for him to wake up and take her into his arms once again.

But, as he was still dead to the world, in the wake of the earth-shattering realisation that she was mad about him, maybe now would be a good opportunity to take stock of her life to date. To think about what she *really* wanted for the future. For herself and her child. She needed to consider her responsibilities and work out her priorities. She needed to figure out why she hadn't been more excited about getting the partnership as she'd always envisaged.

And, frankly, it was about time.

Rolling onto his back, still half asleep, Marcus thought that if the night he'd just had was a dream he didn't plan on waking up any time soon. It had been astounding, and, he suspected dozily, not just because it had been a while since he'd had sex.

Celia had been voracious, he recalled, the images flickering through his head making him smile. And demanding. On the way to her bedroom she'd told him what she wanted him to do to her, blushing fiercely and muttering something about pregnancy hormones. He didn't know about the validity of that, but nor did he particularly care because whatever it was that was driving her desire to almost insatiable levels it had seriously turned him on. They'd combined hot and fast with slow and sensuous, his fantasies with hers, and it had been everything Marcus had imagined.

And everything, he suspected, he'd feared.

Searching for her with his hand and hoping to roll her beneath him before the doubts and fears took hold, when he came up with nothing he cracked open an eyelid. To see she was sitting on the window seat, wrapped in a dressing gown, her legs crossed as she looked out of the window, a thoughtful expression on her face.

He levered himself up onto his elbows and rubbed the sleep from his eyes. 'How long have you been sitting there?' he asked, blinking and noting that the sky beyond was no longer the deep black of night, but the teal-blue of imminent dawn.

'A while,' she said, giving him a smile that made warmth unfurl in the pit of his stomach and his body stir.

'What are you doing?'

'Thinking.'

'About what?'

She gave a little shrug. 'Just things.'

'What kind of things?'

'You really want to know?'

'I do.' He shouldn't, but as things he wanted to think about even less were threatening to invade his head he did.

She swung her legs off the window seat, stood and walked over to the bed. 'OK,' she said, sitting on the mattress and crossing her legs Buddha style. 'Well, first, I'm going to turn down the partnership.'

That did the trick, he thought wryly, shock pushing those creeping thoughts back as he stared at her. 'You're what?'

'I'm turning down the partnership.'

He opened his mouth. Then closed it. 'Why?' he said eventually. 'I thought it was everything you've ever wanted.'

'So did I. But I now realise it isn't.'

'Since when?'

'Probably since the moment they told me and instead of feeling fireworks going off inside me what I felt was more like a damp squib.'

He shoved his hands through his hair and gave his head a quick shake because this wasn't small. This was huge. Worryingly huge. 'Are you sure?'

'I'm sure,' she said with a firm nod. 'I've been so focused on getting it, working so hard and making so many sacrifices, and now I can't help thinking, for what? So I can work even longer hours, more weekends? And end up with burnout, having a breakdown or worse? I don't want to do that. Not any more. It's not fair.'

She rubbed a hand over her stomach and he wondered if she realised she was doing it.

'More to the point,' she continued, 'I don't need to.'

He frowned. 'What do you mean?'

'Most of my entire adult life has been driven by one

thing. Getting my father's approval. And the partnership was tied up with that because I really thought that he'd be proud of me. But I rang him this afternoon to tell him and all he did was bang on about some woman he'd met on the Internet. Whatever I do I doubt I'll ever have his approval and I doubt he'll ever be proud of me. He's just not the type.'

Marcus felt his entire body shudder with the strength of the protective instinct that streaked through him and he suddenly burned with the desire to drive to her father's house right now and shake him until he realised what an amazing daughter he had.

'And you know what?' she added, almost as if she was talking to herself. 'I'm actually fine with that. I don't need his approval. I'm good enough without it. More than good enough. And what's so great about him anyway? He might be a first-class lawyer, but as a human being, as a man, he's pretty pathetic.'

He wanted to cheer and then wrap her in a massive hug, but, a bit baffled by that, instead he said, 'So what are you going to do if you don't take the partnership?'

'Resign, definitely. Maybe move firms, if I can find one with a child-friendly policy. Maybe switch to a different kind of law. Maybe work from home a bit. I'm not entirely sure, but I do know that I don't want to rush back to work the second I give birth. I want to spend some time getting to know my child. I mean, I'll probably go mad after a few months, but at the beginning, at least, I think the time is precious.' She stopped and frowned at him, even as she smiled. 'What?'

'Nothing,' he said, trying to untangle all the emotions rushing through him. 'I'm just a bit taken aback, that's all.' Or try stunned. Confused. Deeply, *deeply* disturbed.

'Not half as taken aback as I am,' she said dryly. 'You were right about my work-life balance all along, Marcus. I do need to change it. I also ought to learn how to cook.

And I'd like to take you up on your offer of the house next door, if it still stands, because you were right about this place as well. I mean, the stairs, the neighbours, all this white immaculateness… Hardly compatible with a messy, crying baby.'

He didn't know what to say to that. How could he retract the offer of his house now? When she'd obviously put a lot of thought into these decisions. These life-changing decisions.

Made because of him. Made possibly because of the night they'd just spent together. Damn, now—too late—he remembered why sex with her was a bad idea. It was never going to be just sex. It was potentially life-changing and he didn't want lives changed. Not hers, especially not his.

'There are a couple of other things you ought to know, Marcus.'

'What?' he muttered, feeling a cold sweat break out all over his skin because one night of spectacular sex and she was turning into someone he wasn't sure he could handle.

'Firstly, I'm in love with you.'

He froze, went numb for a moment before his entire body filled with dread, dragging him down. 'And secondly?' he said, sounding as if he were deep under water. Which maybe he was, because he certainly felt as if he were drowning, because he knew what was coming next.

'Secondly, I think you might be in love with me too.'

The room tilted, spun, and if he hadn't already been lying down he'd have crashed to the floor. He felt sick. Weak. His brain imploding with the effort of denying it.

'I'm sorry, Celia,' he said, his head a mess and his throat tight and the word *escape* flashing in his brain in great big neon letters, 'but I can't do this.'

'Can't do what?' she said calmly.

'This.' He waved a hand between the two of them, struggling to keep a lid on the panic. 'I'm not in love with you.'

She nodded. 'OK, look, Marcus, I get that this has all

probably come as a bit of a shock to you, and I know how
the idea of being in love terrifies you, so if you need to leave,
that's fine. If you need some time to figure out how you feel
and what you want that's also fine. I can wait. Not for ever,'
she said with a soft smile that he didn't understand at all
because he couldn't think of a situation that less required a
smile, 'but I can wait.'

CHAPTER FOURTEEN

'SO WHAT'S GOING ON, Marcus? First you knock up my sister and then you abandon her? On what planet is that OK?'

At Dan's words—spoken so casually, so conversationally and a mere couple of metres to the right of him—Marcus froze. For the briefest of seconds his concentration shook and his foot slipped. His shoulders wrenched and the muscles in his arms screamed and he had to grit his teeth against the sudden shocking pain. Cursing his so-called friend with what little breath he had, he strengthened his grip on the crimps and jammed his foot back into position.

Trust Dan to wait until they were halfway up a wall and thirty feet off the ground before launching his attack. They'd met up around half an hour ago, and at any point since then he could have brought it up, but no, as the owner of one of London's most successful advertising agencies, Dan was all about maximum impact.

'I wouldn't put it quite like that,' Marcus muttered, although that was exactly what he'd done.

'Then how would you put it?' said Dan, swinging his arm up and latching onto a sloper.

Marcus braced himself and hitched himself up a foot and absolutely refused to wince as his shoulder protested. 'I needed a bit of time and space to figure some stuff out.'

'What could take a month?' Dan asked through gritted teeth. 'I only took a fortnight.'

Well, now, wasn't that the question of the century? thought Marcus, stopping for a moment to catch his breath.

Why was it taking so long to work out? As Dan had said, it had been four long, agonising weeks, and he was still no closer to unravelling the mess inside his head than he had been when he'd walked out of—no, *fled,* would be a better description for the way he'd left—Celia's flat.

'Just stuff,' he muttered.

'Ah,' said Dan knowingly, grabbing his water bottle, unscrewing the lid and taking a glug. 'Stuff. Gotcha.'

They stayed there like that for a moment, breathing hard and rehydrating as Marcus tried to figure out what it was Dan thought he knew, until he couldn't bear the thundering silence any longer. 'Anyway, Celia was the one who suggested I take a break,' he said, as if that made what he was doing all fine.

'I doubt she meant quite this long.'

Marcus did too. And that simply added guilt and shame to the chaos in his head. 'Have you seen her?' he asked.

Dan leaned back into his harness and wiped his brow. 'Yup.'

'How is she?'

'Getting big. Looks a bit tired but other than that, fine.'

'Good.'

'She resigned, you know.'

'She mentioned she was going to.'

'And she's started house-hunting.'

Marcus winced, but Dan carried on regardless. 'You know, I knew she was making a mistake thinking you'd stick around,' he said.

Marcus stared at him and nearly dropped his water bottle. What the hell? He *was* sticking around. Of course he was. He was just trying to figure out how. And coming up with a blank because how was he supposed to keep himself safe if he saw her all the time?

'She said you'd decided to face up to your responsibilities and was actually quite strident in her defence of you. But I had my doubts.'

Marcus felt his chest tighten. She'd defended him? When was the last time anyone had defended him? Been on his side the way she was?

'And actually I don't blame you,' Dan continued, 'because being tied to Celia for the rest of your life? That's not something I'd wish on anyone, least of all my best mate.'

OK, that was enough. 'What the hell are you talking about?' he snapped.

'I know I'm her brother, but that doesn't make me blind to her faults. I love her to pieces but she can be difficult. She's stubborn and uncompromising and as tough as nails.'

'She's not any of that,' said Marcus grimly, feeling his heart begin to thump and his head pound.

'No?'

'No,' he said even more grimly.

'Then what is she?'

Fabulous. That was what she was. Brave, loyal, clever, brilliant and gorgeous. The mother of his child and the woman he was head over heels in love with.

As the truth of it broke free from the shackles he'd bound it with, his head swam, his vision blurred, his muscles weakened, without intending to he let go of the wall.

Down he fell. Down, down, down. Jerking to a juddering halt a metre from the ground. Every bone in his body jarred. Every muscle screamed. But his head was clearer than it had been for weeks.

He'd spent the past month trying to work out how to resist falling in love with Celia but what was the point when it had already happened? He might have been in free fall only a moment ago, but his heart had been in free fall for weeks, month, years probably.

He was nuts about her. Well, of course he was, because

how could he not be? She was the most amazing woman he'd ever met and the time he'd spent with her had been the best, most stimulating, fun time of his life.

She was the only woman he wanted to commit to, and not just because she was having his baby. The only woman he could ever imagine living with, loving, till death did them part, which would hopefully be later rather than sooner. They were having a child together, going to be a family, if he hadn't totally screwed things up.

It wasn't the fact that Celia had told him she loved him that had put the fear of God into him. No. That made him feel as if he were on top of the world, as if he were the strongest, bravest, best man in the world.

It was the fact that she'd suggested that he was in love with her. He hadn't wanted it to be true because he'd always thought of love as dangerous. Treacherous. Life destroying and very much not for him.

But maybe it didn't have to be like that. Maybe it could be as lovely as Celia had said. She'd scared the life out of him when she'd told him that he was in love with her, but really what was there to be scared of? Dan seemed to be doing all right.

Maybe when it came down to it, there came a time when you had to stop wallowing in the past and get on with things. Like life. And maybe that time was now.

'Are you all right?' said Dan, who'd abseiled down the wall and was looking shocked and a bit pale.

'Never felt better,' said Marcus, now burning with the need to sort out the utter balls-up he'd made of things.

'Are you sure? No whiplash? Torn muscles?'

The only muscle tearing was his heart, because when he thought of what Celia must be going through because of his thick-headed selfishness it made him physically *hurt*.

'I'm fine.'

'You scared the life out of me.'

'Sorry.'

'That's all right. Anyway it's only fair since I probably scared the life out of you.'

Ah, thought Marcus as it all became clear. His friend, with all his talk of love and marriage happening to him one day, all that nonsense about Celia being tough and difficult and uncompromising prodding him into accepting the truth, was more perceptive than he'd ever given him credit for.

'Thanks, Dan,' he said, lowering himself to the floor and unbuckling his harness.

'No problem,' said Dan with a broad grin. 'First Kit, now you. What can I say? It's a gift. In fact I ought to start charging.'

'Then send me the bill. Right now, though, I need to go.'

When she'd told Marcus she'd wait, Celia had assumed he'd need maybe a week to realise he was in love with her and come to terms with it. A fortnight at the most. But here she was a month after he'd walked out on her and she still hadn't heard a word.

She'd started off so patient, so calm and confident, absolutely certain that she'd done the right thing in putting the 'love' thing out there for him to confront, but as the days had dragged by and he still hadn't come to find her her calm had shattered, her confidence had crumbled and she'd slowly fallen apart inside.

The past week had been agony. She'd thought love sounded lovely, but it wasn't. It hurt like hell. She only had to think of him and she physically ached. Something would happen, something she'd do, and she'd want to tell him. The first time she'd felt the baby kick, the job offer she'd received, the stupid mobile she'd bought for a nursery that she didn't yet have… She'd picked up the phone. And then had to put it down again, her heart wrenching and her eyes stinging.

And while outwardly she put on a good front, catching up with friends, keeping doctor's appointments and house-hunting, her heart had broken piece by tiny piece. Until now there was practically nothing left of it.

Nothing left of anything really, she thought miserably. She was all out of anger at his obstinacy. All out of frustration. And all out of hope.

She'd been so stupid. So naive. Had she really thought she'd be able to defeat his strength of will? Had she really been so arrogant as to presume she knew what he was feeling?

If only she hadn't resigned. Then at least she'd be working, keeping so busy that she wouldn't have time to think about him. But she had, and as a result she'd thought about little else, wondering what he was doing, who he was with, and driving herself mad by going over that last conversation and beating herself up with regret over pushing him too hard too soon, wishing so much she hadn't done it.

But she couldn't change any of it. All she could do was learn to live with it and hope that by Kit and Lily's wedding next weekend she'd have built up enough strength to handle seeing him.

It wasn't as if she'd be able to drink herself into oblivion to get through it, was it? So maybe she'd take a date. If she could find one who didn't mind her five-months-pregnant belly. Maybe she'd hire someone instead. Someone witty and gorgeous and who'd pretend to be utterly devoted to her. Someone who'd show Marcus that she wasn't missing him. Wasn't thinking about him. Wasn't—

The buzzer buzzed and Celia jumped. She cast a quick glance at the clock and frowned. She was going out with friends tonight in an effort to perk herself up, but the taxi she'd ordered was an hour early. Damn. Maybe she'd given the wrong time. A couple of months ago she'd never have made such a mistake but now it felt as if she was making them all the time.

Whatever had gone wrong, she wasn't anywhere near ready. She was still in her dressing gown, make-up free and her hair was still wet. She wasn't going anywhere for a while, so with a sigh she walked over to the intercom and lifted the handset.

'I'm sorry,' she said, 'there's been a bit of a mix-up. Could you come back in an hour?'

'No mix-up,' said the voice at the other end, a voice that made her breath catch, shivers run up and down her spine, goosebumps break out all over her skin and her heart lurch. 'And as I can't wait an hour, or even another minute really, if you wouldn't mind, I'd like to come up.'

Celia's heart began to thump as her head swam and emotions like joy, relief, love and hope began to surge through her. Oh, God, this was what she'd been waiting for for so, *so* long. He was here. At last. And in all the scenarios she'd envisaged she was looking immaculate and composed instead of a washed-out wreck, but it didn't matter. He was here, and that was all that counted.

Unless, of course, he was here to tell her that she'd been wrong, she thought, her heart suddenly plummeting and all those lovely feelings vanishing. That while he'd always be there for the baby he'd never be able to be there for her. That he didn't love her and never would. Because of what happened with his parents. Because he was as stubborn as a mule, because... Well, because of just about anything, really.

Ordering herself to get a grip before she got hysterical, Celia pulled herself together. Whatever the reason he was here she wanted to know, and the only way she was going to do that was by letting him in. So, reminding herself that she'd be wise to keep her emotions in check and her face blank, even if it killed her, she took a deep breath and pressed the buzzer.

Marcus pushed open the downstairs door and felt a wave of relief sweep over him. He was in. That was a start. Now for the hard bit.

He jogged up the stairs, his heart beating hard and fast, which had nothing to do with the energy needed to climb four flights of stairs and everything to do with the woman at the top of them.

Who was standing there, looking neither ecstatic nor horrified to see him, merely inscrutable. And so utterly, gorgeously magnificent he couldn't believe he'd taken so long to realise just how much he loved her.

'Marcus,' she said coolly.

'Hello, Celia,' he said, not fazed by the coolness one little bit because what with the idiotic, selfish way he'd been behaving he hadn't expected anything less.

'What are you doing here?'

'I've come to see you.'

'Clearly,' she said witheringly. 'However, I'm about to go out.'

'Not for another hour.'

She frowned. 'OK, fine. What do you want?'

'How have you been?'

'Me?' she said, looking a little surprised at the change of conversational direction. 'Oh, absolutely fine.'

'And the baby?'

'Fine too.'

'What have you been up to?'

'Well, I resigned.'

'I heard.'

'So I've been relaxing.'

'About time.'

'And learning to cook.'

He grinned. 'How's that going?'

'Messy. I'm a long way off roast beef with all the trimmings, but I'm getting there.'

'I can't wait to try it.'

She arched an eyebrow as if to suggest there wasn't a hope in hell of that, and if it hadn't been for the desire in her eyes, the faint blush that stained her cheeks and the way she was tightening the belt on her dressing gown he'd be worrying that he was too late. That he'd lost her and she'd already moved on.

'I've been offered a job that I think I might take.'

God, he was *so* proud of her. 'Congratulations.'

'Thank you. I've also put an offer in on a house.'

Marcus went still. Well, hell, *that* wasn't happening. 'Withdraw it,' he said.

Her eyebrows shot up. 'What? No. It's in a great location, has loads of space and a lovely garden.'

'So does mine.'

'Huh?'

'Move in with me and let's be a proper family. I love you, Celia. So much. I'm sorry it's taken me such a long time to figure it out, but I adore you. Everything about you. You're amazing and I'm so, *so* proud of you. Our child is the luckiest child in the world to have you as its mother. I should have told you all this that night, but I was spooked, as you knew I would be. Running away was a knee-jerk reaction but I stayed away out of fear, obstinacy, stupidity, and I'm so sorry.'

He stopped, breathing hard, his heart thumping and his blood racing as he watched her, standing there staring at him speechless, as if it was all too much to take in. And suddenly he thought, Oh, to hell with it. The most efficient

way to show her how he felt and to find out how she felt
was to simply march over to her and kiss her.

As Marcus' arms came round her and his mouth descended,
his eyes blazing with everything he'd just told her he felt
for her, Celia melted.

It had been so hard maintaining a cool, stony-faced fa-
cade when all she wanted to do was hurl herself at him and
beg him to love her. She'd so nearly cracked when she'd
mentioned the sensible but soulless house she'd found. And
then he'd said what he'd said and she was still reeling, still
hardly able to believe it.

Was it really true? Did she really not have to be miserable
any more? Could she really let herself believe it?

His kiss told her it was, she didn't and she could, and she
nearly passed out at the happiness coursing through her, filling every corner of her and making her heart beat madly.

'I love you, Celia,' he murmured raggedly against her
mouth. 'We have so much to look forward to. I've spent so
long looking backwards it's clouded my judgement. For far
too long. But not any more. Will you marry me?'

She went dizzy, practically about to burst with happiness. And then she winced and took in a quick, sharp breath.

'What?' he said, drawing back and looking down at her
in concern. 'Too much? I knew it would be too much. Or is
it too soon? OK, we can wait. If that's what you want. I'd
marry you right now if I could, but I can understand if you
have doubts. I mean, *I* know I'm a sure bet but of course
you'd have concerns. Especially when I've been such an
idiot—'

'No, it's not that,' she said, her heart almost bursting as
he stumbled over his words.

'Then what is it?'

'The baby kicked.' She took his hand, and put it on her
bump. 'Here. Feel.'

'God. That's incredible.'

'*You're* incredible,' she said softly. 'I don't have any concerns about you, Marcus. I have no doubts. Because I love you too. You're my best man and you always will be, and of course I'll marry you.'

'Seriously?'

'Seriously.'

He looked down at her. 'Who'd have thought?' he said almost in wonder.

'Who'd have thought?' she echoed softly.

For a moment he looked at her, his eyes shimmering with love and hope and a tiny glint of wickedness. 'So this thing you're meant to be going out to tonight...' he said, tugging on the belt of her dressing gown and pulling her towards him.

Her breath hitched and desire began to surge through her. 'Easily cancellable.'

'Anything else in the diary for the next few months?' he murmured.

'Nothing important.'

'Good,' he said, smiling and lowering his head, 'because we're going to be a while.'

* * * * *